The Tomato Expert
A Tale of Love & Regret

By

Marshall Paterson

For Mary! A Florida Girl Forever.

[signature]

Dark Hearted Dream
Publishing

The Tomato Expert

Dark Hearted Dream Publishing

Flint, MI, USA

Copyright © 2021 Marshall Paterson

ISBN: 978-0-578-98272-4

Front Cover Picture – danchooalex via iStock

Design & Typesetting – Martial Law

This is a work of fiction. Names, characters, places, and incidents are the product of the author's imagination or used fictitiously, and any resemblance to actual persons, living or dead, businesses, companies, events, or locales is entirely coincidental.

ABOUT THE AUTHOR

Scottish born Marshall Paterson has lived in Michigan, USA since 2001, and became a US citizen in 2017. Following the publication of several technical works The Tomato Expert is his first work of fiction.

marshallpaterson@hotmail.com

Let creation reveal its secrets by and by.

After the Deluge – Jackson Browne

He had always known what I did not know and what, when I learned it, I was always able to forget. But I did not know that then, although I learned it later.

A Farewell to Arms – Ernest Hemingway

Chapter One – Strangers in The Night

Even before the two of them came into the house on that first night, I knew full well they would have no idea that I was sitting there, curled up in the darkness on my own. I had heard the familiar sound of two cars easing up into our loose-stoned driveway, and so I was already curious to know who was with my sister since I knew that her boyfriend, Brad, would never come around at that time of the evening on a 'school night.' This was back during the first few days of a long, hot, summer which must be over thirty years ago now that I think about it. Back then I used to love to sit, long into the wee hours of the night, in my father's old leather armchair, and look out of the patio doors onto my mother's little moonlit vegetable garden. So, there I was, as my elder sister and her mysterious guest broke the spell of my solitude. I guess you could say that I was a little bit guilty of spying on them as I curled up even more in my secret place in a deliberate attempt to conceal my presence. However, I seem to have been able to forgive myself for that particular little sin over the years that have passed since.

Mary was almost three full years older than me and, although she tried hard to live up to her role in life as my big sister, I had always thought of her as much more of a 'little girl' than me, if you know what I mean? Not that I was any great sort of a grown-up-woman or anything like that, but Mary just always seemed to be a little bit bubblier and gigglier than me for some reason. Sometimes I even got the impression that she would deliberately play those things up whenever there were other people around. Every birthday gift she ever received was always just "the best ever," and everyone she knew always seemed to be either "so wonderful" or "so fantastic" that no one else could compare. She was like that with Brad too in a lot of ways. He was always such a "perfect" boyfriend if anyone asked her, but honestly, I am not so sure that I ever really believed that she meant it. Not that I didn't adore her, you understand. She was my big sister and I had always worshipped her just for that fact alone. I still do for that matter, and it seems to me that even now, after all these years, we hardly ever go for more than a few days at a time without either seeing or speaking to each other. Back then, in those long-gone days, I sometimes thought that it was only my mother and I who ever saw Mary in any of her rare dark moments, but in the more recent years it seems to me that some of her sorrows have become just a little bit more obvious to the world at large.

The fact that she didn't switch the light on when she came into the house on this particular night was my first real clue that Mary was up to something. When I had heard the cars arriving, I had expected her to be with Pauline, or Francesca, or any one of the other girls from her midweek workout class. I had expected bright light to suddenly flood through the house, and the sound of their girlie chatter to reverberate all around as they made themselves late night snacks and poured themselves oversize drinks, all the time oblivious to the fact that our parents would already be trying to get some sleep upstairs. Instead, I heard whispers, and car keys being laid down ever so gently, so as not to rouse anyone. I couldn't actually hear what was being said when I heard his voice for the first time, but I could tell they were kissing and touching and, just for a moment, I started to feel more than a little bit guilty at intruding upon their private moments. If I'm being honest, I was enjoying eavesdropping on them, and I was more than a little bit curious about what was going on. I was still only catching a word here or there, but I did hear her whisper "No, we can't!" I remember thinking to myself at that moment, 'No Mary, you can't, but you want to.'

I suppose that I had occasionally wondered about Mary's private life back then. I guess that it was just part of my role as her little sister to be curious about her. I do distinctly remember the day that my mom took her to our family doctor to get her put, "on the pill," as everyone used to say back in those days. It was another one of those little rite of passage moments that our mother always seemed to revel in, like the day she took us for our first bra, or when we had our first period. Sometimes I think those little watershed moments meant more to our mom than they ever did to either Mary or me. On the day of their visit to the family doctor they had come home like a couple of co-conspirators who had a huge secret that they couldn't ever share with anyone, even though I knew the pair of them could never hope to keep it to themselves. My mom was almost giddy with excitement, and she kept going on and on about how our dad must, "never find out." I always thought that was funny, given that our dad was the least catholic of any of us, but at the time I didn't really understand that any objection on my father's part would have had nothing to do with any of his religious beliefs. My sister herself wasn't nearly as excited about that day as our mom seemed to be, and I actually think that just the thought of them having a secret together might have been more important to Mary than any imaginary sense of freedom that birth control was supposed to give her. For some unknown reason, I had gotten it into my head that Mary and Brad never actually did any of that sort of thing anyway, even though they had been a couple for so long.

Now, sitting there in my little secret place and listening to her yield to this voice in the dark, her giddy, childish manner seemed to disappear, and it was like I was overhearing, not only a man that I didn't know, but also a young woman that I suddenly didn't really recognize. As I say, I had felt a little bit guilty at listening in on their conversation, but for some reason I had no such qualms about overhearing their love making. It was almost as if I regarded their shared words as somehow more sacred than their intimacy. To this day, I still have no idea why I felt that way and that's a huge part of the reason why, even now, I could never let Mary know that I was sitting there in the dark that night.

Hiding in the shadows and overhearing them finding each other for the first time, I had no idea that her guest was just this ordinary kid that I had already seen around town on occasion. It wasn't until the following afternoon when he showed up again that I recognized him. He was one of those kids you would see in town, but you never really knew who they were. I would occasionally see him with a few of his friends in either of the two bars that everyone used to hang around in back in those days. I didn't recognize him at all from high school, and so I would have assumed that either he was a little bit older than me, or that maybe he'd gone to some other school. Of course, that was all on the assumption that I had given him any thought at all, which, as I'm sure you can guess, I hadn't. One thing for sure is that, prior to that day, I certainly could not have told you his name was James.

I myself wasn't in either of those two bars all that often of course, mainly because I was a little too young at that time, and I could only sneak in occasionally as part of a crowd, or when one of the doormen took a shine to me. A bar wasn't the type of place I really wanted to go to regularly anyway to be honest, although the thrill of being in a "grown up" place could sometimes be pretty cool at that age. Mary too only went there occasionally, even though she was legal and could come and go pretty much as she pleased. When she did go to the bar, she usually went with one of her girlfriends. She and Brad never went to the bar together as far as I can recall, and they hardly ever went out to eat together either. I remember her telling me one time that she preferred to go to the movies with Brad because that way she didn't have to talk to him. I laughed of course, but I suppose I did also feel a little bit sorry for him because at that time he struck me as a nice enough guy, even though he seemed to have had some sort of a personality bypass. I guess that I too found conversation with him to be hard work now that I think about it. Looking back, maybe it was Mary that I should have felt sorry for, given that I knew how she really felt about her so-called "perfect" boyfriend?

As for James, well, I guess no one would really consider him to be a particularly good-looking guy, but then again, he wasn't exactly hideous either. If by good-looking you mean "tall, dark, and handsome", then he pretty much let you down on all three of those qualities. It wasn't that he was particularly short or anything like that, but you certainly didn't have to look up in order to look him straight in the eye. You could tell that he had been one of those kids who had had the blondest of blonde hair when he was a toddler, but who had lost that bright appearance as he had gotten into his teens to the point where now you weren't sure whether to describe him as blonde or not. He didn't help matters much by constantly looking like he was a few weeks behind on when he ought to have visited his barber, although that was one of very few areas where he didn't seem to pay all that much attention to his appearance. Like the rest of him, his face was thin, and he had just a hint of cheek bones that he ought to have played up a little with a sharper hairstyle, but his lips were thin and almost indistinguishable in color from the rest of his face, and his jaw line was maybe just a hint too long for him to qualify as ruggedly handsome. One thing I did notice about him right from the start was that he never wore t-shirts, or anything else for that matter, which carried any type of legend or logo – whether it be an allegiance with a particular rock band, or a sports franchise, or even a favorite type of beer. The brand labels on his clothes too, if there were any, were always small and discreet like he didn't want them to be noticed. Looking back, I sometimes wonder if that was just down to random chance, or whether he was actually smart enough at that young of an age to have thought it through, and he was trying to persuade the world to listen to what he was saying, rather than just judge him by his appearance?

That following day, I had come out of the shower, and I could hear voices downstairs in the huge open space that was the center of our childhood home. Mary was just managing to get an occasional word in here and there, but it was my mother's voice, and the voice of my sister's guest that I was hearing the most often. Once again, I couldn't hear exactly what they were saying at first, but when the piano started to play, my curiosity got the better of me and I started to make my way downstairs to see what was going on. Here was this kid sitting at the old baby grand piano that our dad had said would make a great centerpiece for the room, even though no one in our house could actually play a note. I guess none of us knew that the piano even worked properly up until that very moment. He was playing short snatches of pop songs from the 1960's and 70's, and our mom was loving it. He would sing a little bit too, but in a sort of comically exaggerated way that kind of caught the feel of the song without ever being note perfect. It was almost like he was caricaturing or slightly mocking the original singer and song. I noticed too that he never played a song all the way through, and I was starting to wonder if he even could.

My hair was still dripping wet from the shower, and I was dressed in only my favorite raggedy, old silk paisley-pattern robe, so I wasn't really ready for the world at that particular moment. As a result, I just sat down on the very top step of the stairs overlooking them and didn't say a word. He must have played maybe another half dozen short snatches of songs before Mary finally caught sight of me and said "Maggie, this is my friend James". He looked up at me as I sat with my knees pulled up to my chin and said simply "Hi" as I raised my hand in a little silent wave back at him. He started to play some piece of classical music which I recognized right away but which I couldn't tell you the name of if my life depended upon it. It was the only thing that I ever heard him play all the way through from start to finish. I never saw the significance of that at the time, and maybe I'm reading a little bit too much into it now too.

Looking back, I think the one thing that took us all by surprise in those first few days that James was around our home was the fact that our father seemed to take to him so well. My dad had never really paid all that much attention to what he referred to as our "little boyfriends" over the years. He always seemed to either completely ignore, or be clearly dismissive of, any of the kids that either Mary or I brought home. One thing for sure is that he certainly never took Brad all that seriously. I can't recall a single time when our dad ever invited Brad to take part in any of the things we were doing as a family.

Officially our dad worked as an "antiques dealer" and for sure, he was able to provide very well for us over the years. Now that I know a little bit more about it however, it is clear to me that not everything he did was always 100% legal. He had a shop in the west end of the town where we lived, but even from an early age, it was obvious to me that it could never bring in enough money to cover its costs and provide the lifestyle we enjoyed. Looking back, I am guessing that the store might actually have been a bit of a cover for whatever it was that he really did to make his money. Of course, neither Mary or I knew anything about any of those things at the time, and even now it is still not completely clear to me just exactly what our father did for a living. I'm not so sure that our mom even knew either, although I suspect that in her case, she might have deliberately chosen not to know.

I could see the look of surprise and pleasure on Mary's face that day when our dad invited James to go shooting with him. Officially, Brad was still her boyfriend at the time, and he would be again when all of this was over, but here was this new boy being invited to get involved with Dad on maybe only the third or fourth time he had been in the house. Maybe it was the fact that James was the type who spoke up and had something to say for himself but, whatever the reason, I could see how our father always seemed to be listening to everything the boy said, and that he was turning it over in his head before he would make any reply. James was honest enough to admit that he had never actually shot any type of a gun in his life before, but that he was happy to give it a go. For a brief moment Mary looked like she was expecting to be invited to go along with them, but in her heart, she knew that this was one of Dad's "guy things" and she would be staying home with us while the men folks went to the shooting range.

Even in my young mind I always had a very clear impression of what the shooting range was like. In my imagination, I could clearly see this place where our father would go, and I could see all the people he would meet. His friends in the club were all familiar to me; Donny, Bud, Frank, and all the other bit players who made up the full cast of characters in my dad's social life. In truth however, I have no real idea of just how accurate my vision is because none of us ever went with him to the shooting range, and none of us ever actually met any of these characters. Well, except for Bud that is. My mother and I were fated to meet with Bud one day.

James was not exactly dressed in the most appropriate manner for a trip to the gun club, in his jeans and denim jacket, but off he went with our dad leaving Mary, mom, and me, to wonder what they would talk about as they drove together. For some strange reason, it wasn't in the slightest bit surprising to any of us when Dad invited James to stay for dinner when they got back a few hours later, even though I remember thinking at the time that if he'd invited Brad to eat with us it would have been the first time in all the years that he and Mary had been together. None of us knew all that much about James' background at the time, and we still don't for that matter, but his immaculate table manners were clear for all to see as he joined us for that first meal. Although I thought that it was pretty interesting for a kid who never gave us the impression that he came from a particularly well-to-do background to be so well mannered, the one thing that struck me more than anything else was how completely comfortable the boy was in referring to my mother as "Catherine" right from the outset.

Mary spent the rest of those summer months playing her little game; pretending to visit James for "piano lessons" while she was still dating the "wonderful" Brad. We all knew better of course, or at least all of us except maybe Brad himself. He might have been blind to what was going on, or he might even have chosen to be blind to it but, at the end of the day, he was the only one of us who got to the other end of that summer unscathed. By the time we had gotten through the fall of that year and on into winter, you could see the difference in Mary. The little girl tone in her voice was gone and she no longer had that overly enthusiastic attitude which I had occasionally found to be just a little bit distracting, almost to the point of being annoying. I don't think you could say that she was any less happy within herself after that summer, but she was certainly much more mature, and she was clearly in the early stages of morphing into becoming a next generation version of the classic lady that our mother had always been. Mary was also much less dismissive of Brad in those days after that summer with James, and she started to defend him a little bit if either me or Mom would run him down at all, no matter how playfully. Out of the blue one night it was Mary herself who asked Brad to stay for dinner, not long after we had seen what we assumed would be the last of James.

Chapter Two – Home and Homecoming

As you can probably guess, Mary never practiced any of her supposed piano lessons at home, and I highly doubt that she even could. Now that I think about it, none of us ever heard James play again after that first time either. Yet, for some reason, I could never imagine myself not mentioning playing the piano in any description that I might ever make of the boy. Like a lot of things, I sometimes wonder if my memory of that first and only time he played for us has become somewhat clouded or sentimentalized over the years. Sometimes, when you re-live a particular set of events over and over again in your head, you end up beginning to believe a version of the story that is really your preferred recollection, over what might have actually happened. Whatever the truth of the matter, it's still the case that our mother never lost any of her enthusiasm for the boy even after everything that went on later had all played itself out. My mom certainly seemed to be completely oblivious to any feelings that Brad might have had about the matter, and all summer long she was forever inviting James to stay for dinner, while the unfortunate Brad waited patiently for his first seat at our table. At the time, I think I began to entertain the notion that perhaps my mom had decided that James was "the one" she wanted for Mary, regardless of what her daughter herself might have felt about the matter.

I remember one particular Sunday afternoon when Brad's car drove up in front of our house while Mary and James were standing together in the covered doorway at the front of our home. Brad never even stopped his car as he saw them standing there, and he disappeared just as quickly as he had arrived. Mom and I couldn't help but laugh and tell Mary how she was "so busted", but she brushed it all off, safe in the knowledge that she would have no difficulty in clearing things up with Brad later. I wasn't quite sure what to make of the defiant look on James's face at that moment, and you certainly couldn't say there was any suggestion of him being embarrassed or concerned about getting "caught", that's for sure.

The old piano itself stills stands in our mother's house to this very day. Like the rest of us, it's showing its age a little bit and has picked up a few more battle scars along the way, but it has found a new role in life as the place where my mom will lay out all the papers she has to deal with on her own these days. The piano was one of those things that my dad had bought with a view to moving on quickly at a decent profit, but which ended up staying with us forever. Lots of the other things in our house had a much more temporary residence of course, as we basically lived inside what was effectively little more than an extension of our father's stock room. Dad would arrive home with some item with which he was going to make a "killing", but which would then hang around for a while until he was finally able to find any kind of a buyer at any kind of a price, and then it would be gone just as we were beginning to get attached to it. That was something that always seemed to fascinate James. He had a knack for noticing every new item that would show up in our house, and he always seemed to be able to point out some feature it had or give us some kind of backstory behind it that no-one else knew. James also seemed to have an unnerving ability to notice any items that had disappeared from our home since his previous visit, and then plaintively lamenting their departure. I'm pretty sure that was one of the things that our father liked about him; he would chat with my dad about all his acquisitions, and he always came across like he knew what he was talking about. I remember one particular day when my dad had brought home a large format print of a Turner seascape, in quite an expensive looking picture frame, that he had gotten from some random estate sale that he had wandered into. James was talking about the picture, and he was giving us his take on what it all meant, mentioning all kinds of symbolism and the like that I myself never really understood. In the meantime, it was clear that, up to that point, our dad had it in mind that it was only the ornate frame itself which had any realistic resale value. I had no idea whether the tale that James was spinning us was his own original BS, or if it was just something that he had plagiarized from elsewhere, but it did all sound pretty plausible, and my dad was just eating it up. In my mind, I could envisage my dad repeating the self-same story verbatim to any potential buyer and, in the process, coming across like he himself was some kind of an art expert. You only ever needed to tell my father something once, and then he could repeat it word for word, almost as if it was something he had always known.

Just a week or two after James first came on the scene there was one strange day when Mary, Dad, and I, were driving back from visiting our grandmother on my father's side of the family. I can't remember why, but my mom wasn't with us that day for some reason. That was actually a pretty unusual situation because our mother had always gotten along so well with her mother-in-law and the two of them loved to visit with each other, almost to the point of excluding everyone else in their raucous conversations. On this particular day, we were passing through a neighboring village on the way home after the visit when Mary said randomly, "That's where James lives" as she nodded in the direction of a small stand-alone, single-story home, set just a little way back off the main road. Without saying a word, my dad stomped violently on the brakes to stop the car, almost like he was avoiding a crash, and barely a minute or two later we were knocking on James's front door.

For a guy whose clandestine girlfriend had just turned up at his door unexpectedly, with her shady father and her little sister in tow, James couldn't have looked more relaxed. He didn't seem to be in the slightest bit surprised to see us and he was already pouring drinks for us within a few seconds of inviting us in. Mary knew her way around the place pretty well from what I could see, and she was completely relaxed and comfortable the whole time we were there. She sat in the corner of a couch with her discarded shoes on the floor and her legs tucked up underneath herself sipping from her glass. Dad didn't say all that much, but I could see him looking around the place taking it all in. He was laying back in the center seat of another old couch that was backed up against the wall opposite the only window in the main room. He still had the little cigar he had been smoking in the car, and he seemed to have no qualms at all about continuing to smoke in his young host's home. Dad would crack the odd witty remark now and then and do that thing where he would exhale smoke and laugh at the same time in one of his little signature mannerisms, almost like it was the process of exhaling smoke itself which was funny. Mostly though he was quiet, and he let Mary ramble on while he just continued to cast his experienced eye around the place. I'm guessing that he thought that none of James' stuff was worth any great amount, even though it was pretty interesting to look at. He had framed prints of famous works of art all over the house, although it was obvious that they had all been cut out from magazines, calendars, and the like. Our mom would have loved looking around his place despite the fact that there wasn't a single-family photograph to be seen anywhere. She would have latched on to any of those she had seen, and she would have used them to try to tease out even a brief version of a family history from the boy.

As I recall, there was music playing on a pretty decent looking hi-fi system of the type that was popular back then, and for some reason the vision of the bright blue display on the front of the tape deck, pulsing in time with the music, sticks in my head. I can't recall what the actual music was, but I do remember being surprised by whatever it was at the time, and I also remember that he made no effort to turn it off, or even lower the volume, when we came in. I've gotten it into my head that he did that deliberately in response to my dad's decision to keep smoking his little cigar because, other than that, you would have to say that the boy really was one of the most well-mannered of young men you could hope to meet. His place was a lot cleaner and tidier than I would have expected a young single guy's home to be, but the furniture itself was old, and it certainly didn't give you the impression that he himself had chosen it. I guessed that maybe he rented the place furnished, and I did kind of enjoy trying to decide for myself which of the items in his home were his own, and which belonged to his landlord.

As always seemed to happen back then, I found a way to wander around in what I thought was a completely unnoticed way while the "grown ups" talked. I'm sure I looked at his place with a completely different eye to the one my father had been casting. I could see that James had been reading "The Old Man and The Sea" before we arrived, and he had laid the book face down, open at his page, next to an old copy of a magazine for shooting enthusiasts. I noticed there was a mailing label on the front cover of the magazine which let me know that he had probably stolen it from the waiting room of his dentist. I couldn't help but smile to myself at the thought that he was at least making an effort to learn about guns and shooting, even though the front cover showed a picture of a country gentleman in a Barbour jacket with his shot gun in hand, looking nothing like either James or my father. The only time the boy engaged with me during the whole time we were there, was when he handed me the drink that he had prepared for me. James didn't seem to care that he was handing me alcohol with my father watching, although I did wonder how it was that he knew I was a white wine drinker when I could get away with it?

To my mind, the only thing that looked to be of any real value in the whole house was a spectacular looking guitar which was prominently displayed in the corner opposite the door in the main room, and which seemed to almost float on an elaborate looking wooden stand. It was one of those old guitars that can't seem to make up its mind about whether it's an electric or an acoustic model, and that might have been used by a Chuck Berry, or a BB King, or one of those guys. My dad didn't even notice it as far as I could tell and so, less than an hour after arriving, we were back in the car and off on the last leg of our journey home. I was wondering if perhaps my dad had decided that there was nothing of any real value in James' home, and I wondered how much that might change his regard for the boy from that point on. Mostly however, I was wondering if I was the only one of us that had noticed there wasn't a piano anywhere to be seen in the house.

One thing I do distinctly remember about that particular day is that my mom was standing at her easel painting when we finally made it all the way home. Our mother taught art in the same local high school that Mary and I attended. She was pretty good at most crafts, and she even kept a potter's wheel in the basement which she would fire up every once in a while, but painting was her first love, and her one true lifelong passion.

I always had the impression that for her, teaching kids to paint was something she had gotten into as a temporary measure while she continued to try to develop her own artistic style, in the hope of being discovered one fine day. Like a lot of us however, when her passion became her occupation, she seemed to lose something along the way. Occasionally she would have a burst of creativity and turn out four or five new canvases in short order, and our dad would admire each one in turn and say, "Oh yes! This is the one". It never was "the one" of course, and so her paints would lie idle again for maybe another month, or a year, or until whenever the notion came over her once again. It was not until this very minute that I have given any thought to the possibility that having James' youth and enthusiasm around our family at the time could have been the catalyst for that little burst of artistic activity on the day we arrived back from my grandma's house.

I always like to think that our mother was quite well liked and well respected as a teacher in our school but, of course, it's hard to be sure when it's your own parent that your fellow students are talking about. The boys at school certainly liked her well enough because she had maintained her looks and her figure much longer than most women of her age, and Mary and I were both fortunate enough to inherit whatever gene it was that let her spend her whole life in that slim, waif-like look that a particular type of man seems to appreciate. If Mary and I were being honest, however, we would have to admit that our mother had more poise and class in her little finger than the two of us had put together. She wore heels and a dress every day of her working life, looking like quite the sophisticated lady, and without even the slightest hint of being the tease that I'm sure the all the boys would have loved her to be.

I do sometimes think that maybe my sister suffered just a little bit in her high school years from being the daughter of one of the school's high-profile teachers. I guess that maybe it's the case that a lot of people will have the expectation that the children of academics should automatically be amongst the strongest of students. Unfortunately however, my sister wasn't ever able to back that expectation up. At best she was an average student, and she also struggled to find either a creative or a sporting talent to compensate for her academic limitations. She was one of those kids who never really "belonged" in high school, but who was never deliberately or cruelly excluded either. I certainly don't recall her ever having any enemies during those formative years, and no one was ever even mean to her, but her friends were all as equally low-profile as she was, and so she sort of flew under the radar, to the point where her high school years passed off without any real teenage drama. My parents did a great job of never putting too much pressure on Mary to succeed in the classroom just because of my mom's position in the school, and I'm pretty sure that part of reason my folks played down my own successes in high school was to help Mary avoid feeling even the slightest sense of failure. They were just as supportive when she made the decision to go straight into the workforce rather than going to college when she graduated, and so it was that she took a job working in a small privately-run children's daycare center out on the far edge of town. Occasionally I would hear her describing her role at the daycare with maybe just a hint of exaggeration, but it was clear to all of us that she was very much a "helper", rather than a childcare professional. That's not to say that the kids she worked with didn't love her or that she wasn't devoted to them too. In a lot of ways, it was the perfect job for her where she could exploit her caring attitude and get something in return that couldn't necessarily be measured in the dollars and cents that she earned. In the first Fall after she started working at the daycare, she signed herself up for some evening classes in childcare at a nearby community college, and we all got the impression that she had found her vocation and was hoping to make a career of it. Things never really turned out that way until much later however, although I'm sure that Mary did learn a lot of things in those days that made her such a great mother when her own time came. I always envied her for that. I might have been the one who had the education, the career, and the so-called success, but it was Mary who was the one that mastered the art of being a parent better than anyone else that I ever knew.

Mary had gotten involved with Brad in her high school junior year. At what seemed like the very last minute, Brad had asked one of his friends to ask her if she would be willing to be his date at the school homecoming dance *if* he asked her. Mary tried hard to play it down but, in reality, she was just as excited about the invitation as our mother was, and I'm sure that some of the pain of having sat at home in her freshman and sophomore years began to be assuaged just a little. I was pleased for her too of course, but I did take something of an initial dislike to Brad even though I hadn't even really met him at that point. There was something that kind of stuck in my throat about the fact that he had used a friend to be sure that he would get a 'yes' response from her before he would formally ask her to be his date. Looking back of course, it's clear that he himself was just as low-profile and lacking in confidence as Mary herself was, and that he too needed to protect his fragile ego like so many other kids do at that stage in life.

Even though mom and Mary only had a few days to get themselves organized, they still did a great job of packing in all the excitement and anticipation that a mother and daughter would have had if they had all the weeks to prepare that a more conventional invitation would have provided. Enough dresses were considered and rejected before the "perfect" version was selected, hair and nail appointments were made and confirmed repeatedly "just to be sure", and a professional makeup artist was hired just in case anyone thought for one moment that this wasn't a big deal. To be fair, my sister did look beautiful on the day, and she seemed to have captured at least some of my mom's poise and elegance, to the point where I could see her confidence growing with each pointed-toe step that she took. On the other hand, it was no surprise to anyone that Brad wasn't nearly as able to carry off the formal look, and that he seemed to be completely uncomfortable in his ill-fitting tux, even though someone had helped him to make sure that the waistcoat he was wearing was a perfect matching color with Mary's ice blue dress. I'm sure I wasn't the only one who didn't hear him speak a single word all the time that my mom was shooting off roll after roll of 35mm film on her old Pentax camera, before the young couple set off for the dance itself. Brad's expression was locked in an almost permanent grin like he couldn't believe his luck at how well Mary had risen to the occasion. He had the same look on his face the next day when he showed up unexpectedly at our door to ask my sister if she wanted to go walking with him, and a full-on romance that never really ended until they divorced many years later was born.

For me, I suppose that the highlight of that year's Homecoming was, not only seeing my elder sister finally become much more of a part of her school community, but also the thought that this would free me up for my own future a little bit too. Brian Chapman was a high school senior that year. He was a kid that was pretty big in the school baseball and basketball circles, as well as being on the football roster, and I suppose you would say he was one of the more popular kids around the school. He had asked me a number of times to go to the Homecoming dance with him that year and, although I desperately wanted to, I told him that my mom wouldn't let me go because I was only a freshman at the time. That wasn't even remotely true of course. In actual fact, our mother would have loved that I too had gotten invited to the dance, and she would have given me just as much attention as she ultimately gave to my sister. It was just that I myself wasn't sure that my mother knew exactly how Mary had felt staying home from the dance in those previous two years. Sometimes you have to let your big sister be your big sister, just so that you can always be rightly regarded as the little sister.

So it was that I was quite happy to spend Homecoming alone that particular year. Mom and dad took off somewhere just like they did most Saturday nights, and I spent another overly long time in the hottest shower I could stand, before wrapping myself in nothing more than that old robe and climbing once more into dad's old chair, enveloped in the scent of his cigars and the worn leather of the chair itself. I remember sitting there wondering who Brian Chapman had chosen for his date in my place without even the slightest touch of jealousy as I waited for darkness to fall. For me there was always something about nighttime that was much more appealing than any other time of day. Sometimes I'll hear people debating about whether a particular friend of theirs is a night bird or a morning person, but with me there was never any doubt in their minds. My mother would always tell me that even from my earliest days I would be awake much more often in the evenings, and I would set aside my daylight hours to catch up on my sleep. It seems that even as a baby I was always content to be awake at night, although I apparently never raised the whole house with any of the nocturnal tears and cries that many young parents complain of. The night that I had sat there listening to Mary and James together for the very first time was a far from an unusual situation for me. Even in the winter months, when mom's little garden was buried under a blanket of snow, I would be more than happy to sit there in that smoky old leather chair looking out on the scene.

There is also something about the darkness that, for me, seems to somehow amplify every sound that an older house will choose to make when it suspects that no one is listening. I would hear the refrigerator in our kitchen humming it's one note song all night long, while the pump in the basement would join in every once in a while, just to keep it company. Occasionally the old wooden stairs would creak just a little bit without any foot upon them to justify the interruption, and oftentimes I would hear a clicking, ticking noise as our heating system cooled down for the night. Sounds from outside the house would fascinate me just as much. If I heard a car passing by in the darkness, I would wonder who the occupants were, and where were they going at that time of night? I would find myself building quite a backstory for them in my imagination as they set off on their nocturnal journey. The sounds of the trains on the tracks a mile or two from our home were few and far between compared to their daytime schedule, but for some reason I seemed to notice them much more after dark. There was something about the darkness that made them sound even further away than they really were. For all that I learned to love all these sounds in the night, none of them came close to being as precious to me as the way that I loved to hear the soft murmur of my parents' voices as they lay awake talking to each other at night. It only happened occasionally, and please don't get the impression I was overhearing them being man and woman, because it was never anything like that. It's just that once in a while I would hear the soft lilt of my mom's words followed, much less often, by the deeper tones of my dad's replies. These were conversations that I actually *felt* much more than I really *heard,* because I'm pretty certain that I never made out a single word in all the times I overheard them. None the less, for me, it was very reassuring to know that they were just as awake and active as I was, albeit that they didn't have my glorious sense of solitude to enjoy. For my part, I like to think that the very act of hearing all these things, which I assumed most other people would miss, taught me the fine art of personal silence, and I have often prided myself on an ability that I believe I have developed, that lets me come and go all around the house, in the wee small hours, without anyone being anywhere near to being roused, or even aware of my presence.

As I look back on that first Homecoming success for Mary, I don't why it was that I never really took to Brad all that much. There was the fact that he didn't have the nerve to ask Mary himself for the date, of course, but that's hardly a reason to hold the kind of lifelong disregard that I can't help but have for him. Other than that one particular thing, there was nothing you could really say that was actually wrong with the kid, so I couldn't say that I had a reason to dislike him, but then again, I didn't have any real reason to actively like or admire him all that much either. Maybe that was the problem; he was the type of kid that didn't really stir any strong feelings in me either way. Mary and I were always very close growing up and Brad could never hope to change that, so I certainly never felt threatened in any way in that respect and, though he eventually became an almost constant fixture in our house, I never ever felt like he 'stole' my sister from me the way some siblings do in that type of situation.

I suppose you would have to say that he was fairly good-looking kid, certainly more so than James in the classical sense I guess, but again, not exactly god's gift to women either. He was on the taller side, with a thick shock of jet-black hair that he wore in a neat style which he had cut every couple of weeks to the point where it never seemed to change in the slightest. His skin was clear enough by the time he and Mary became an item, but I do remember from seeing him around the school that he had suffered from a bad case of acne a year or two before they got together, and I always associated him with that even long after it had cleared. He wore a standard teenage uniform of blue jeans and t-shirts, and the closest that he ever came to rebellion was when he took to wearing a "Gun'N'Roses" t-shirt to school long after the cool kids had moved their allegiances on to other rock bands. In high school, Brad had been a strong academic student by all accounts, but he didn't capitalize on it when he graduated, preferring to stay home and go to a local college while passing up the offers he had from better schools further afield in the process. He was a math major in college, which pretty much tells you all you need to know about him right there. Later on, he took a job with one of the big banks on the trainee managers track, and I'm sure he could pretty much see his whole life mapped out in front of him by the time he was around 23 or 24 years old. Of course, this was back in the days when banks would consider steadfast guys like him to be a prize catch for their recruitment program, but I'm also sure they already regarded him as a little bit of a dinosaur just a few years later when they began to recruit the kind of shark the world of finance came to prefer.

Brad and Mary finally got married about a year and a half after my dad got out of prison. The wedding was a classy but understated affair that Mary herself set up and organized from start to end. It certainly had her style stamped all over it, and although my parents would have been more than happy to finance a typical 'big day' for her, she chose instead to go for a low-key event. I think that suited her personality perfectly well to be honest, and I never got the sense that she was deliberately choosing not to flaunt our parents' wealth for fear of anyone remarking about where the money might have come from.

Chapter Three – In the Garden

I only ever saw my mom kissing James that one time. We had all gone to one of those craft fairs that were held in the hall of the church that stood on the opposite side of the street from the old hotel on the way out of town. Dad had tried to tell James that this would be a "girl's thing" and that maybe the two of them should go shooting instead, leaving us women folk to go alone. James was having none of that however, and he insisted that he wanted to go and that it would be fun. In the end we were all shocked, once again, when Dad said that he would come with us too. When we actually got there it was Dad, of course, who was the most into it. He had that whole "eagle eye" thing going on, looking out for a bargain, or for something that he might be able to pass off as being worth more than it actually was. At the time, I didn't think anything of mom constantly referring to James for what he thought of this or that, and it didn't seem at all unusual that they would discuss at length some random item of bric-a-brac that no one else cared about in the slightest.

Back at the house afterwards Dad had asked James to stay for dinner, then suggested he should come sit with him in the den and watch the day's sports news on the TV, while we girls did the cooking. Once again, James was having none of that idea, and before long he was up to his armpits in the kitchen with the rest of us. Mary took off to the store to pick up some "vital" missing ingredient that would make the meal "just perfect" and, after the initial flurry of activity, I retreated upstairs to my own little island of splendid isolation. I had heard my mother and James heading out of the back door and down into the garden to pick the vegetables and herbs they would need, and at first I could still hear them talking to each other. Then, maybe it was because it had gone so quiet for a few minutes that made me get up and move to deliberately look out of my window over-looking the hothouse below.

Mom was wearing a red and white floral print summer dress with a deep cut neckline that would have shown off her cleavage if she had had any to speak of. The skin on her arms seemed to glow in the early summer light shining through the glass onto the pair of them, and she looked for all the world like she had somehow gotten instantly younger in that very moment. Her long curly hair, which she colored back to its original strawberry blond, was being held delicately up behind her head in both of James' hands, while their lips were locked firmly together in a passionate, yet still tender, embrace. James let her hair fall and lowered his hands slowly down her body before sharply pulling the skirt of her dress up to her waist. Mom broke off their kiss and pulled him close into her neck as she threw her head back. If her eyes had been open she would have been looking straight at me.

I'm not exactly sure what my plan was as I made my way downstairs to talk to dad. Perhaps I was hoping to occupy him long enough to prevent him from asking where they were, or perhaps I was hoping to give mom enough time to complete whatever it was that she had in mind with the boy. Either way, in the end, I didn't have to engage dad in conversation at all to keep him at bay. He had a half-full glass loosely held in one hand, and his little cigar in the other, while his arms laid along the armrests of the chair he was reclined in. As always, he would let out his short little combined laughs and exhales, as he watched four or five talking heads on the TV clashing over the outcome of the day's sporting events. He didn't say a single word to me, but I stood there none-the-less, just in case I needed to protect him from his own innocence in the same way as he had always done for me in the past. I watched the cigar smoke drift slowly around him, and I can still smell it now along with the scent of the smooth brown leather from our favorite old chair.

Mom was amazingly cool when she stepped back through the door into the kitchen. Her dress and hair were immaculate as usual, and she was so talkative and relaxed that I started to question myself over what I had seen. For some reason I admired her even more than ever in that moment as she laid her vegetable harvest down on the cramped work top without missing a beat. The forbidden fruit behind her didn't say a single word as he followed her in, and dinner passed off just like any other, although I couldn't help but notice my mother lay her hand gently on James' shoulder at one point as she reached between him and Mary to lay a dish down in the center of the table. As her elegant slim fingers took on an even more porcelain white appearance against the dark navy background of the cotton polo shirt he was wearing, James slowly lifted his eyes from his plate and looked directly across the table at me.

When dinner was over, we all went out into the little garden with our glasses still in hand to enjoy the last of the early summer evening sun. This would have been one of those very rare occasions that my father ever ventured out into this part of his domain. Just occasionally he would wander out to the garden and watch mom as she worked, but most of the time he didn't get any further than the door itself where he would angularly lean his shoulder against the doorframe and hold his little cigar at his side as he surveyed the scene. I don't ever recall him lending our mother a hand in the garden itself, and I guess I never gave any thought to the fact that all the heavy labor in creating mom's little paradise in the first place, must have been done long ago by someone other than my father. Yet, for all that, my mother still turned to him for advice on gardening, even though it was probably the one thing in life that he knew the least about. Maybe that's just the way it was with couples from my parents' generation? I suppose our mom just assumed that Dad knew everything about everything, and I suppose that he thought it was part of his role in life to behave like he did. The outcome here was that my mom's little garden grew into a picture-perfect representation of her constant sense of indecision, and my father's need to be seen in a traditional, head of the family, type of role.

I wouldn't be surprised if a lot of people thought that our parents were an unlikely looking couple. I myself never thought so, but who is ever able to look at their parents with the eye of an outsider? To me they were just Mom and Dad. I suppose that everyone considers their own parents to be "normal", and that it's everyone else's parents who are the strange ones. Up until I began to learn more about how my parents came to be together, I had never really given all that much thought to how different their backgrounds were. My mom was an only child whose own parents had been fairly well-to-do by all accounts. My maternal grandfather owned a printing business that serviced the other local industries with letter heads, business cards, and other office stationery. He himself had been a printer when he had started out, but by the time I knew him it had been many years since he had had to scrub the dried ink from his fingers at the end of the day. He employed around twenty other local men and women, some of whom were the parents of my school classmates. His wife worked in the art department and maybe that's where the roots of my own mother's artistic background lay. You could never say that my grandparents were rich, but as the owners of the business they did pretty well compared to a lot of folks in the town, and my mother obviously grew up in relative comfort. I think her father loved his business, but not so much that he didn't find it easy to suddenly decide one day to sell the whole thing off, lock stock and barrel, and for him and my grandma to retire into the sun, leaving behind quite a distinguished looking young lady in their only daughter.

In a lot of ways, it's clear that my dad's upbringing couldn't have been any more different from my mom's. He was the middle child in a group of three with an older brother and a younger sister. He always used to tell us about how poor they were, and I have no reason to suspect that he ever exaggerated. His favorite story was to tell everyone how it wasn't until he had dinner at the home of his future in-laws that he understood the concept of leftovers at the end of a meal. I never really knew my grandfather on my dad's side, although in the old black and white photographs I saw of him he had the same stocky, cruel looking build that my father had, but with the wearied look of having carried a much heavier burden down a much longer road. My paternal grandma outlived her husband by at least thirty years. She was one of those big personalities who treated everyone the same no matter their background. If she was ever intimidated by the relatively wealthy background of my mother then she never gave any indication of it, and the two of them got along very well in spite of their apparent differences. I believe it was her mother-in-law that led my mom into her lifelong passion for gardening. By all accounts, my grandmother grew foodstuffs as a matter of necessity in the early years of raising her family, but she continued the practice even when things became a little easier for them. I think that my mother admired her for that, and her own gardening was, in some ways, a little tribute to the woman who had raised and nurtured her husband.

On the other hand, in all the years since the summer that James was part of our lives, neither Mary nor I ever really developed the gardening habit.

There will be times, however, when we will find ourselves lamenting the quality of the produce in the local supermarket and then smiling to ourselves as we recognize the real root of our concerns. Mom herself has never given up her garden, although she needs all the help she can get with it these days. At one time she had a little ramp built and she would wheel my dad's chair outside on fine days so that he could be beside her in those first few months after what happened to him. Of course, he couldn't offer her any of his "advice" anymore, but maybe she thought that just having him there would let her feel his influence. She started to paint once again in those days, and it seems that she finally found a style of her own to the point where she would exhibit and sell her work, albeit on a relatively small local scale. It's hard to admit that you don't particularly like your mother's style of painting, but that is the truth of the matter if I'm being honest. For me, I preferred the work she did before she found her own sense of vision for some reason. These days she'll laughingly pass those early efforts off as "derivative", but I'll often find myself looking through her older work whenever I'm able to visit.

My dad had never had the patience to be able to watch her paint in their early days together, preferring instead to look in on her occasionally as the work took shape, or to wait until it was complete. Later on, of course, he had no choice but to watch each stroke of her brush as he sat mute and motionless in his wheelchair that my mom had carefully positioned so that she could keep an eye on him while she worked. I remember one time, maybe just a year or so before he died, that I showed up at the old house to find the place deathly quiet; maybe because there weren't any grandkids around just yet. I saw my mom out in the garden, with her easel set up and my dad in his wheelchair beside her. She was sitting on an old wooden folding chair, taking a break from her painting, and she was having a one-sided conversation with my father just as if he was the same man as he had been in his prime. As usual I didn't announce myself, preferring instead to listen in on what she was saying. After a minute or two, my mom stopped talking and reached into the worn wooden box that she used to house all her painting gear. She pulled out a low flat tin of what turned out to be little cigars, and she expertly lit one using an elegant slim lady's lighter, with the appearance of one of those old black and white movie stars who could make smoking look like the height of sophistication. Finally, she placed the little cigar delicately between my dad's lips. There was a short pause before I heard the familiar sound of him exhaling and coughing lightly at the same time, and I felt a delicate sad smile slide quickly across my face before it was gone.

Chapter 4 - Family Secrets

That summer with James in our lives was right around the same time that Mary had gotten involved in what felt like the start of the great health and fitness movement that persists to this day in a seemingly never-ending series of new trends and fads. Once or twice a week, she and a group of her girlfriends would head out to the gym, or the "studio" as they insisted on calling it, to take part in whatever exercise style was the current height of fashion. For me, it always felt a little bit strange to think about Mary in an enclosed indoor gym setting in the middle of summer because she had always been such an outdoor type of person. I came to realize however, that she was enjoying the social element of these events as much as anything else, and I was pleased for her that she was starting to "belong" to some sort of a crowd at last. I suppose I was a little bit guilty of mocking them all to be honest, but in those days of brightly colored leotards, leggings, headbands, and big hair, it wasn't difficult to see the funny side of things; even though this was a look that suited Mary well with her natural curls and permanently slim build. Perhaps for the first time, she found herself at the leading edge of a trend, and I'm sure that added to her growing sense of confidence.

My Mom too had her own little workout area hidden away in the basement of our home, and in many ways that tells you a lot of what you might need to know about her. She was never the type of woman who would work out in a group situation, and the idea of her getting all hot and sweaty in an open living room environment in front of a video tape playing on the TV was never going to happen. Now that I think about it, I can't imagine that any one of us ever saw her like that. Certainly, we might hear her stepping it out or jogging on her treadmill, but that was as far as it ever went. You never actually saw her in her work out mode. Even once she got done, you never seemed to see her until she was completely ready for the world again, and then she would reappear all freshly showered and ladylike once more. It's almost as if she had developed the art of gliding past us completely unnoticed as she moved between the basement and the shower room upstairs. There was a little bit of that mentality in Mary too and, although some of her friends would show up at our house already decked out for the gym, my sister preferred to travel in her everyday clothes and morph into her workout girl persona only once she was safely within the confines of the locker room, well away from whatever unwanted gaze she might have been trying to avoid.

Mary always knew that my contribution to the family domestic workload was to take care of the laundry, and so I wonder if she ever gave it any thought that I would quickly notice when her workout gear stopped showing up in the old-fashioned wicker basket that I would carry downstairs from her room, past mom's little studio, and on into the little dark washroom in the far corner of the basement? She probably didn't even give it a moment's thought to be honest, and any fault is much more likely to be mine, given that I was being a little bit more observant than perhaps I really should have been about my sister's private business. If I had really been as smart as I sometimes like to think I am, then I might have already noticed that she had started to say that she was meeting the other girls at the gym rather than having them stop by to pick her up like they usually did, but it wasn't till I realized that I hadn't put any of her workout gear in the washing machine for a couple of weeks that it clicked she was leaving the house with her sports bag over her shoulder, and then heading somewhere completely different.

Right away I assumed that her occasional visits to James' place for imaginary lessons on his non-existent piano were no longer enough for her, and she needed to see him so much more often that she had prepared this slightly elaborate little deception. In truth, I was excited for her in a strange sort of way, because it was more than a little bit out of character for this girl who had always been so strait-laced in the past. If I'm pushed, I might even admit to having been just a tiny bit jealous of her, given that I was starting to quite like this boy myself and here she was having this secret life with him. I suppose that I was also just a little bit hurt too, if I'm being truthful. Mary and I had always been so close to each other in the past, and we had shared more than a few of our secrets over the years, so maybe it wasn't all that surprising that I found myself wondering why she couldn't bring herself to share anything of these new adventures with me. Obviously, I was worried about my mother too. There had always been times when the three of us would talk to each other more like sisters than mother and daughters. Part of me thought that all these new secrets meant that it could never be the same anymore and I mourned its passing but, given what I knew about this boy and our mother, I'm glad that Mary chose to keep it all to herself since then I didn't feel at all bad about keeping what I knew to myself too. Once again then, it came to pass that I would spend ever more of those summer nights curled up in my father's old leather chair, with the faint scent of his cigars hanging in the air and looking out on my mother's neatly tended little garden while trying to work out just exactly what was going on in this boy's head.

Occasionally I will hear a random friend say that they think that fall is the best time of year. Or maybe someone else might say that, for them, it is spring that is their favorite of the seasons. I can never be sure if I really believe any of them because I could never understand why anyone might think that any season other than summer was the highlight of the year. Certainly, for me, there was never any doubt. Back then in my high school days, it was always the case that from the very first signs that winter might be coming to an end, I would start to look forward to the long hot days to come, and while spring was pleasant enough and always seemed to do a great job of teasing us with what lay ahead, I couldn't help but wish that it too would pass quickly, in the same way that I always hoped that winter would be both short and mild. In the end, it always seemed to me that spring would stick around for a little bit longer than anyone wanted, like an unwelcome guest at a family celebration.

I remember the small group of tall trees that provided the seclusion to my mom's garden, and how I would watch for the first buds to appear around April time then check them each day to see if they were any closer to bursting open and adding flesh to the tree's thin skeleton which had stood there bravely all winter. Those trees were sneaky of course, and they always seemed to wait until your back was turned for a moment before unleashing their transformation upon the world and so I would find myself asking 'when did that happen?' when I realized that they were already in full bloom.

I didn't think about how important those trees were when I was young of course. In those days they were just another part of the world that I grew up in. Now however, I can see that as their leaves started to come alive each year, they would shut out any view beyond the garden and help us to secure the splendid isolation that our little family had come to enjoy. There was also the cooling effect that their shade would provide us when high summer finally rolled into town, and they would even do their best to extend our summer by shielding us from those first cold snaps when the fall would try to remind us that winter was waiting in the wings again. And so it was that we would spend more time out there in my mom's domain than I suppose a lot of families might have done. If my mom was at all worried that we might have disturbed her carefully tended garden with our youthful play when we were very young, then she never gave us any indication of that, and if we were indeed ever to undo any of her work, she never made a fuss about that either. So, her garden became the place that Mary and I were most comfortable as young children. I think the same can probably be said for Mom herself, for not only was this the place where she would "tend to the land" and paint her pictures in the open air, but it was also where she would lie and read for long hours in the sun, clearly transported elsewhere via the words on the pages that she would turn with clockwork regularity.

As you might well imagine, I have never spoken to anyone about my mother's episode of passion with young James until this very moment. It's one of those slightly sordid little stories that I've always felt the need to keep tucked away in a secret place where only I can find it. Thinking about it now, I suppose that all families probably keep secrets from each other when they think it's the right thing to do. I suppose too that many other people might have far more practical motives for keeping secrets, beyond it just being the "right thing to do". For me, the big problem is that I've never really believed that anything in this whole world can truly be kept a secret from everyone forever. As a result, I have often found myself acting out little scenarios in my head regarding how I will deal with things when certain situations arise given that I believe eventually, all of our secrets will become common knowledge.

In a lot of ways, I suppose I'm probably being a little bit too hard on my mother and father with the attitude that I'll occasionally find myself adopting when it comes to some of the things that I have come to learn about them over the years. I suppose I'm not at all convinced that they really set out to deliberately keep their secrets from us, as much as I'm sure they might have wanted to avoid having to relive certain parts of their past. I guess they just came from that generation where some things were never talked about. Truthfully, I really wasn't all that upset about the details of their backstory when I came to know my mom and dad's history much better, but equally truthfully, I suppose that it does still sting me just a little bit when I think about the *way* that I came to know them as people in their own right, rather than as just my parents. That, and the fact that I couldn't help but feel a little bit let down that those other members of our family had long known what I only came to learn later in life. I don't know for sure that it would have been easier for me if my parents themselves had told me, but it sure does feel that way.

I must have been around 14 or so – a few years before we knew James - when I first learned that my mom had been engaged to another man before she had married my dad. We had all gone to my cousin Cynthia's wedding to her first husband Jack. Cynthia was the daughter of my father's elder brother, and she was only 19 when she got married to Jack, pretty much against everyone's advice from what I can tell. The wedding was a fairly low rent affair held in the community hall of a town about ninety minutes' drive north of where we lived. We hadn't actually gone to the church service in the afternoon, or to the little dinner afterwards for that matter, but we were all invited as evening guests. The community hall was a kind of run-down affair that looked like it had been built in the early 1970s without ever having been remodeled in the intervening years. My over-riding memory of the place is that there seemed to be wall signs everywhere reminding the members and their guests of some random rule or other that had been ordered "by the committee" and which could lead to "suspension of privileges" if it was contravened.

In spite of the rather sad atmosphere surrounding the whole affair, my father's family always knew how to have a good time, and the combination of the music, the dancing, and the drinking, all added up to a great night out. So it was that I ended up sitting at an orange-colored, Formica-topped table with Cynthia's younger brother Stephen, who was a year or two older than me, and who was pretty darn handsome in an old fashioned "bad boy" sort of a way. I guess that him and I had danced together more than a few times when we finally sat back down and tried to recall just exactly how long it had been since we had last met.

They say that families only come together these days for weddings and funerals, but as I was only in my early teens at the time, I suppose that I just hadn't been to enough of those events to really pick up on the full family history. I suppose too that it was all the talk about family weddings, and weddings in general, that led my cousin Stephen to ask me if I had ever wondered what life would have been like if "Aunt Catherine" had married "that other guy". I'm sure that he could tell immediately from the blank look on my face that I had no idea what he was talking about. At the time, I had no sense of the fact that instead of feeling any embarrassment about having put-his-foot-in-it, he was actually starting to enjoy both my ignorance and my discomfort, but for sure I can see that now as I look back. For some reason, it would have been even worse for me if I had come to find out later that my sister Mary had known all about this already, but I was saved from that humiliation when her and I talked about it later and I learned that she too was just as much in the dark as I was. As a result, I have often wondered if maybe it burned Mary just a little bit harder to know that her little sister had found out before she did that our mother had previously been engaged to her high school sweetheart, and that their wedding was only a few days away when the whole thing was called off because of our father.

It was a good number of years later before I was finally able to speak with my mother about those days. I learned that her former fiancé's name had been George, and that they had dated each other all the way through high school and on into their college days. She even shared a few photographs of him that she had kept hidden away, although I found that I didn't have the courage to tell her that George reminded me a lot of Mary's boyfriend, Brad. Mom smiled slightly sadly when I asked her if she had called the wedding off because of dad, before she confessed that it was actually George himself who had brought things to an end after he had discovered her and dad together. I tried to be cool about her confession and I muttered something stupid about men being much less tolerant of that sort of thing back in those days. Mom's sad smile became a gentle laugh at that point, and she said sweetly "Oh it wasn't so much that I had been with another man that bothered him, as much as it was that I had never even been with him at the time. George just wasn't the type of boy that you loved the way I love your father".

Naturally enough, my mom wanted to know how it was that I had come to learn about her past, and when I told her that it was my cousin who had told me that she broke it off, she went on to tell me how that was the "public" version of the story that was told at the time. "George told the world that I had broken things off with him because I wasn't sure about getting married. At the time I was very grateful to him, and I thought he was being such a gentleman for not telling everyone about how he had found your father and I together. Of course, now that I know a little bit more about how men are, I can see that it wasn't really my honor that he was protecting as much as it was his own male pride that was more important to him".

While it was my handsome cousin Stephen that had dropped the slightly scandalous backstory of my parent's romance upon me, it was his father, my Uncle Isaac, who was the one that came to tell me a little more about my father's murky past. Of course, I was a good deal older before that whole story started to unfold, and the summer with James in our lives was a few years behind us by that time. Still, it seems to me that with every family secret that I have learned over the years, I've developed an insatiable curiosity to know what else is there that someone else might know that I don't.

As Mary was playing her little game, I spent the summer that James was around working in my father's antique store in the west end of the city. It was the last long break before my senior year of high school, and for some stupid reason I was struck with the notion that it would be kind of cool to have a little bit more money to spend, and to do something a little bit more "grown up" with my time, rather than just hanging out with friends or laying out in the sun as it seems I had done every other summer up to that point. I convinced myself that working in Dad's store would be fun, not just because there wouldn't be that much actual work to do, but also because it was located in the best part of town, where the old world of all the antique stores met the youthful vitality of the local university community. I hadn't decided yet where I was going to go to college when I graduated from high school, far less make any decision about what to study, but I already preferred to hang out in this part of town over the bars and clubs out where we lived. Even in the long summer break, there would still be a lot of students around, and they would often wander into the store to look around before leaving without having bought a single thing. I'm still trying to work out why it is that young college students seem to be drawn to old world bric-a-brac.

I had worked in my father's store occasionally before that particular summer, but never for any real length of time. My dad himself was hardly ever there, so I guess he was off doing whatever it was that made the real money we lived on, and the store itself was managed on a day-to-day basis by a woman that he had employed for as long as I could remember. Her name was Marie, and it's only looking back now that I realize that I have no idea what her second name was. Marie was a little bit older than our mom, although you certainly wouldn't know it from her dress sense. She had a glamorous look that was verging on borderline slutty, with plunging necklines that showed off her enormous bust, and a penchant for high-legged, high-heeled, boots at almost any time of year. She was quite a jolly character too, and I liked her as much as I liked anyone from her generation, especially when she let out that deep growling belly laugh of hers', usually at one of her own edge-of-decency jokes. Occasionally I would play with the notion that my dad kept her around because she was so much worldlier, and such a visual contrast with my mom, but I never thought there could be anything more to it.

I'm not sure how much Marie really knew about antiques, but when a customer who looked like he had money to spend came into the store, she could play the part of the sexy, educated sophisticate, to a tee.

Customers like that were few and far between however, and there would often be days when the money we took in must have been far below what was needed just to pay the bills and Marie's salary. Of course, I didn't realize all that then, just as I didn't realize that my dad was paying me way more than this type of work would usually command in the real world. My job, such as it was, was supposed to be as a sales assistant, but I can't recall all that many occasions when we had more than one potential customer in the store at the same time, and so the only occasions that I ever actually sold anything were when Marie was on her lunch break, or when she didn't think that a particular customer was going to spend any money at all. For the rest of the time, I mostly just hung around and kept Marie company, but I did rather fancy myself as the creative type, and so I would spend hours collecting and arranging the stock into what I thought were little 'collections' that worked well together, and I would get a particular kick when a customer bought more than one item from any of the little arrangements that I had set up. Maybe it was in this area that I had picked up on my mother's artistic streak? Either way, I do like to think that I have a little bit of a flair for putting things together in a coordinated fashion, whether it be the clothes I wear, the way I layout my home, or even just those little displays in my father's old shop all those years ago.

Once or twice a week my dad would wander into the store late in the afternoon and send Marie and I home early. Looking at the store's books afterwards, it appeared to me that it was on those occasions that all the high value sales were made since the hand-written sales ledger always had a ton of new lines on it on the mornings after he had made his late-in-the-day visits. I assumed he was just writing up all the private sales he had made on the road during his trips, but now of course, I question how many of those sales were real at all. Don't get me wrong, I'm not trying to say that my father was some sort of master criminal who could mastermind complex financial deals. Far from it. Whatever it was that my father really did, it was strictly small time where people might occasionally have gotten a little bit hurt, but no one got killed that's for sure. I guess that's part of what made it so hard to deal with the situation when those guys beat my dad half to death about a year or so after Mary and Brad had gotten married. The thing about it is, we were all pretty sure that they really didn't mean for it to go that far. We all thought at the time that they were just trying to tell him that his days in this business were over, and that he should quietly make the decision to "retire". Unfortunately however, in trying to send him that message, they denied him the ability to ever again make a decision about anything.

Chapter 5 - Hard Time

I'm guessing that the lead up to what ultimately happened to my dad began a year or two earlier when the phone calls started. It was obvious right from the outset that something bad was going on, but most girls at that age trust their daddy in a way that they never do again in later life, and so I just ran with it. My father knew fine well that I would be home alone when he began to make those calls and I, in my turn, worked out right away that for some reason he wanted it to be me, and me alone, who would answer when he rang. My mom had told Mary and I that he was "away on a business trip", which wasn't all that unusual at the time, but something in her manner in sharing this with us this time around seemed to say a lot more than the words themselves did. Or, at least, it did to me. I never knew if my sister suspected that there was any more to it, because by that time the days when her and I would talk about everything were already in the past, and we never discussed the matter. So it was that I would be home alone in the late afternoon as the phone would ring, and when I answered my father would ask me flat out if anyone had been at the house looking for him. So, I knew right away that he was in some sort of hiding, but I also knew he was never going to tell me what was really going on. The calls were always short but not sweet, and he made sure to end them all with a clear instruction not to mention to my mom or my sister that he had called, then he would tell me that he would see us all soon enough in a tone that never gave me any doubt that he would, even though you might think it would be a little bit hard for me to believe because of the nature of his question and the nature of his calls. Of course, I was more than a little curious, and very concerned, about what was going on, but I knew my father well enough to know that there was no point in my even asking for an explanation. Truthfully though, I spent more time trying to work out why father chose me, the youngest of the family, to be his source and his confidante. I was torn between believing that it was my youth and innocence, against my growing belief that my father felt that I understood more than we ever discussed in words, and that it was me rather than my sister or my mother that he could rely on to do the right thing when the time came.

He didn't call every day, and never on the weekends, and for the first ten days or so I was always able to tell him that no, no one had been looking for him, but then the police had shown up that Monday morning asking for him. They were as evasive as my father himself would have been when mom asked them why they were looking for him, and so she said nothing more than that he was away on a buying trip around the country, visiting various auctions and private home sales. She went on to tell them that these trips would normally last anywhere from ten days to a month depending on how things went for him. That's when it first struck me that just maybe my mother knew a little bit more about my father's business than I had always given her credit for. She delivered her lines with a level of conviction that even had me believing her when, in reality, I knew fine well that my father had never spent any more than one or two nights at a time away from his home and his girls in the whole time we were growing up. Dad never gave me any indication whether he was happy with my mom's handling of that situation or not when I told him about it, but when he went on to ask me whether the police officers had been uniformed or plain clothes, I could hear his little signature laugh combined him exhaling his cigar smoke at the other end of the line, as I let him know that it had been two young guys in full uniform.

What I couldn't tell was whether my dad was more, or less, concerned when I went on to tell him about his friend Bud's visit on the evening following the morning that the police had shown up. I had gotten home pretty late that night, and I was a little bit surprised to see a strange car in the drive that immediately put me on edge given the current circumstances. I certainly didn't recognize the car, and though I didn't really pay all that much attention to it at the time, I do remember thinking that it looked both expensive and new. When I got inside, my mom and this man were standing on either side of the fireplace which was crackling and sparking away nearly as much as the atmosphere between the two of them. Mom was still dressed for work in an elegant dark navy, high-necked dress, and heels, which served to exaggerate just how short and stocky her heavyset guest appeared to be. He was wearing a suit that looked almost as new as his vehicle, but which gave him the distinct impression of being the type of guy who couldn't admit to himself what size he really should be wearing. The buttons on the jacket seemed to be straining to keep his body in check. For all the slightly comic look this gave him, there was no doubt in my mind that there was something slightly sinister about this guy. Mom had a completely confident and defiant look about her that I don't think I had seen before that night or on any other occasion since. Looking around, I couldn't see any glasses or coffee cups to suggest that this had been an amicable meeting. The two of them continued to look straight at each other as I laid down my purse and hung up my jacket on the old coat stand beside the door. If any words were spoken between them I certainly didn't hear them until my mother broke off her gaze and addressed me saying "Maggie, this is your father's friend Bud from the gun club. He was just about to leave." Bud continued to look straight at mom for a second or so before turning towards me for the first time and bowing his head slightly, then turning slowly on his heel, and taking his leave of us. I never heard him speak. My mother too, didn't say a word as we listened to the strange car leaving our driveway, but then she said rather matter-of-factly, "I'm going to step into the shower," and I knew that this was my cue that the conversation was over, and I shouldn't even think about asking her anymore. The next day, when I was relaying these events to my father, he said nothing more than "Bud? That's interesting." That was to be the last time that he called before he reappeared at home a few days later, acting as if nothing had ever happened, and leaving me in the dark with another family secret that I knew but didn't understand.

So it was that I don't suppose any of us could honestly say we were all that surprised when my dad went to prison, although it certainly didn't soften the blow in any way. For such a long time it seemed that he would get away with whatever he had done, and then, even when they found him guilty, the judge still sent him home while he reviewed the background reports making us all think that our father had dodged a bullet, and that he would get ordered to pay restitution, or maybe some probation time at worst. After all, the amount of money they convicted him for wasn't all that much in the great scheme of things, and it seems that no one had gotten hurt in the process. So, we had ourselves convinced that they wouldn't want to waste the taxpayer's money by sending a man of his age to prison for the first time. In the end, being sentenced to a year and then coming home after eight months, wasn't nearly as bad as it might have been, but things were never the same in our family after that.

In the run up to the trial, my dad had kept the whole thing very quiet and not even mom, Mary or me really knew what was going on, other than he was in a "bit of trouble". I guess he was hoping that he wouldn't get sent to prison and so no one would really need to know what was going on. When they let him come home while they prepared the background reports, he too was convinced that he was free and clear, and so he never made any further plans for what to do if he did have to be gone. On the day of his final court appearance for sentencing, I got home from work only to find mom, Mary, and Brad sitting eating in silence at the breakfast bar. When I walked in, my mom just looked straight at me and said, "A year". The only thing I could think to reply was "Fuck!"

Once cooler heads began to prevail, we sat down to talk about what to do next. My grandmother was still alive at the time and so she had to be told that her golden boy had run into some difficulties. Given that she was the one major concern, the three of us considered all the options while Brad contributed absolutely nothing to the discussion as usual. In the end it fell to me to drive north to let Uncle Isaac know what had gone on, and to ask him to be the one to break the news to his mother about his baby brother. For some reason, on the ninety-minute drive north, I couldn't stop thinking about anything else other than the fact that Brad was a useless piece of crap, and I couldn't believe my sister was going to marry him.

Uncle Isaac was great, and he couldn't have been more understanding when I arrived to tell him about his brother being incarcerated. He seemed to appreciate that I had come all that way to talk to him in person, rather than just making a phone call, and he appeared to get a kick out of the fact that it was "baby girl" who had been dispatched to deliver the message. If only he knew.

Sometimes I'll find myself wondering what my Uncle Isaac really thought about the way things had played out then, and in the years that were to follow. Here he was, the older brother and ostensible head of the family, living in a rundown home, driving a beaten up used car back and forth each day to his dead-end job, while his poorly educated kids made a seemingly never-ending series of bad decisions. Meanwhile his 'golden boy' baby brother was so successful and living in the neat home of a self-made man, with his independently wealthy wife, and enjoying all of life's little comforts. Perhaps my Uncle Isaac found the time to smile to himself a little bit as he turned the key in his old beater car and started the long drive down state to share the bad tidings with his mother. I, for one, wouldn't begrudge him such a smile.

So it was that I headed home again, safe in the knowledge that my uncle would deal with the issue of breaking the news gently to our grandmother. I also returned home with the new knowledge that this wasn't the first-time that my dad had gotten into a little trouble with the law over money. It seems that in his late teens there had been some deal with "bad checks" going on, and that my dad had been called to court to answer for his actions. As always with my dad, he had tried to keep the whole thing to himself, but my grandfather had apparently managed to get wind of what was going on, and so, on the day of the hearing, both my Grandpa and my Uncle Isaac had shown up unexpectedly in court and spoken up on my dads' behalf, offering to settle the issue and to take responsibility for the young miscreant's future conduct. It seems that the judge was so impressed that he went for it, and the family went home fully intact, albeit a little lighter in their collective wallets. I'm not sure why, but for some reason I found myself liking all three of them even more after hearing that story, even though I never actually met my grandfather.

If I'm being honest, I've got to say that those eight months on her own while my dad was gone were actually pretty good for my mother. She started to develop the independence and self-sufficiency that would stand her in such good stead after dad got hurt, and I think she also started to rediscover a little bit of her identity independently of her husband. I don't want to give the impression that she liked being on her own, but it is the case that in a lot of ways it allowed her to remind herself of just how strong a woman she was in herself.

My dad, as you might well expect, was never quite the same man afterwards. When he did finally come home, he somehow looked smaller and less imposing than before, and he had certainly lost a lot of his confidence, although whenever he met anyone, he always started the conversation with that defiant look about him like he was just waiting for them to call him out as a crook before he pounced on them.

Personally, I never really had any problem with my dad's occupation in as much as I knew about it, and in some ways, I might even have admired him for it. I didn't feel the slightest bit of shame when he went to prison, and although I didn't exactly broadcast it to the world, I didn't keep it a secret from anyone either. In the days immediately after he was sentenced we all just seemed to get on with the practical issues of dealing with all the mundane things that my dad would normally handle, including the fact that it became clear that our mother had never paid a bill in her life before. Once those first days were behind us however, we still never found the time to sit down as family and talk about who this man we only knew as a father and husband really was. As a result, I really have no real idea how my mother or sister feel about the fact that my father was a minor criminal who got caught. Maybe that's all because we really didn't know a whole lot of the details, and that we probably never will. When I think about it now however, our father did a great job of protecting us from that side of his life, and I'm sure that most people looked at our family, and the two innocent girls our dad had raised, without the slightest suspicion about what was really going on.

Maybe another reason that Mary and my mom didn't want to talk about it was that they had the same slightly guilty feeling that I myself had about being secretly quite proud of what my dad did? It's not exactly the right thing to say these days, but I actually had the feeling that there was something quite manly about his lifestyle. I've often wondered why, with the liberal outlook and so-called modern thinking that I shared with my mother and my sister, I still had that sense of my dad being a man's man, and my loving him all the more for it. I suppose that I might actually have gotten my sense of what masculinity is from my father himself. He was proud of the way he had gone about making himself into what he considered to be a success, and he had that whole masculine thing going on that allowed him to believe he was more of a man than many others, just because of the way he had gone about it. Why then, should I be at all surprised that I had inherited a little bit of that misguided mentality from him? I clearly remember one day back in that summer with James when I found a moment to ask my dad what it was that he liked about the boy. He didn't even have to think about it as he replied that "James looks like the type of guy who can take care of himself." I remember the slight shudder that ran through me as I realized what those words meant. Maybe it wasn't a shudder at all? Maybe I should be honest and confess that it was actually a thrill that ran through me at the barely suppressed suggestion of violence playing a part in my father's regard for the boy?

I don't suppose I'll ever know for sure if Mary felt the same way about my dad's lifestyle as I did. Although she and I were still very close, that's not the sort of thing we would talk about anymore, and I'm not sure she could really express it properly to me if she tried anyway. I'm not even sure that I could either, for that matter. For my mother, on the other hand, I have no doubts about how she felt. It would have been right around the time when James was on the scene that I started to wonder what it was that brought my parents together in spite of the sharp differences in their backgrounds. But that was also the time I was starting to learn about my dad's lifestyle, and so I'd find myself looking at him and knowing exactly why my mother had thrown her lot in with him.

Chapter 6 – Alone with The Boy

Although my father's trade meant that most of the furniture, and a lot of the other items, in our house had only a temporary stay, the basic core and style of the place remained fixed all the way through my childhood and is still relatively unchanged to this day. In a lot of ways, you could describe our home as being quite a dark place. Most of the walls were painted in bold but rich colors, with the whole of the downstairs area being a deep red shade in our own little version of The Red Room. The floors were all dark polished woods with rugs rather than carpeting, and although the ceilings were high and the windows tall, my father's preference for dark woods and rich colors worked to prevent anyone ever getting the impression of a light, airy space. It's a retro style that has become somewhat fashionable among the well-to-do folks these days, but back then everyone else lived in homes with pale colored fitted carpets, and white pine furniture that gave them an open, light, slightly stark, Scandinavian look. Our house, on the other hand, always had an overwhelmingly busy look about it. There were times when you would struggle to find an open place on any surface to lay something down upon, and the concept of "a place for everything, and everything in its place" was not something that counted for much in our family.

The downstairs area was almost completely open plan with the kitchen, the dining room, and the den all opening onto the main living area. The only doors led onto the downstairs bathroom, the basement, and to a curious little office area where our dad would while away many hours whenever he finally gave up on his favorite old leather chair in the den. The fact that he kept the office door locked on a pretty much permanent basis obviously gave Mary and I a huge sense of curiosity about what lay behind the door. Whenever we played outside as very young children, my sister and I would clamber up to office window from the garden below and try to shield our eyes from the reflection as we peered into our dad's secret place. I recall we would invent elaborate stories about why we were excluded from this part of the house, although I'm not sure that any of our fictions were very much stranger than what the facts might have been.

The basement area belonged almost entirely to my mom and was the second-best kept part of the whole house after her bedroom. She had her potter's wheel set up down there along with her painting area which was the best lit part of the house in an attempt to simulate being outdoors, I suppose. She also had her little workout area, which she had set up long before it was fashionable to exercise, and she had some beautifully fitted wardrobes where every item of clothing she ever owned was meticulously stored in pristine condition, ready for her to bring out each of her "collections" as the seasons changed.

Like much of the rest of the house, the stairs from the main living area up to the bedrooms were of a dark wood and a reassuringly solid construction. They wound up around two right angle bends onto a long galley-like hallway with a view down onto the living space on one side and the bedroom doors on the other. Mary and I shared the large upstairs bathroom at the top of the stairs which our mother always made sure was nearly as well-kept as her basement area. Each of the four bedrooms was painted in a different color to the point where we referred to them by their color rather than by the name of the occupier. Mom and dad shared the pink room with its own bathroom. I always thought it was a bit of a misnomer to call it the pink room because, for me, the color was verging on purple, giving the room a certain royal feel to it. Mary was in the green room, which was the smallest of them all but which she didn't seem to mind even though she was the older sister, and I was in the blue room at the end of the hallway with my view out onto the garden. Occasionally we would have overnight visitors who would be relegated to the sterile white room that took on the double duty of being a guest bedroom and the place where my mom would lay out her carefully chosen outfits for the next few days.

Until I met him last week for the first time in over thirty years, the only occasion I had ever spoken to James alone and for any length of time, was that day he showed up at the house when Mary got delayed at the daycare. There was some problem with a couple of kids not getting picked up on time by their over-stretched parents, and so Mary had to stay behind to help look after them until their folks finally showed up. Given that this was in the days before cellphones, Mary had phoned home to let me know that James would be coming around, and she asked if I would be good enough to let him know that she was going to be late, and would I keep him occupied till she got there? I was a little bit surprised at myself when I began to realize that I was looking forward to his arrival and having him all to myself for a little while. It could be that I might be deluding myself, but I got the impression that maybe he felt the same way too, when he arrived at the door just a little while later and I told him that it would just be the two of us for the time being at least.

Right off the bat I thought he looked sharp as he stepped through the door. This was way back in the days when the current fashion faux pas of a denim jacket with perfectly matched faded blue jeans would still have been considered a cool look, especially along with the predominantly red plaid shirt he had paired them with. I distinctly remember asking myself how he managed to wear the collar of his jacket turned all the way up without looking like a complete ass, but I checked myself as I suddenly realized that I was looking at him a little bit more closely than was probably healthy for either of us. Still, I couldn't help but notice how well manicured his nails were, or that the brown leather watch strap was a perfect match to both his belt and his boots, which had a certain 'working man chic' about them. He turned down my offer of coffee in favor of hot tea which, in the end, turned out to be a blessing because the aroma of the coffee might have over-powered the scent of his gorgeous woody cologne that I caught onto as I leant over to pass him his cup. I wondered if he'd applied it specially for my sister or whether it was part of his everyday routine. Either way, that was one thing he got perfectly right.

I suppose most people would say that James did look pretty good naked. Like I've said somewhere before, he wasn't exactly god's gift to women in terms of his general looks, and his most noticeable feature was probably just how downright ordinary he looked. Maybe that's why he took such care with his dress sense? Personally, I'm not a huge fan of the male nude to be quite honest. I have always thought that the male body was a lot more functional than aesthetic, and I myself don't really know what the fascination is for those women who salivate over the "body" models we seem to see more and more of in the media these days. Fully clothed, James could only ever be described as skinny, but disrobe the boy and he instantly became somewhat more athletic. Not only that, but he seemed to immediately become a little bit taller too as his legs appeared to lengthen, pulled longer by their sharply defined muscles. A little bit of a tan and some flattering lighting seemed to highlight his stomach muscles, while his chest was smooth and hairless in a way that any of those body models would have been proud. He had a tattoo at the top of his right arm long before it became popular amongst young men. It took the form of a tall ship on a wild blue sea, and you can be sure that it had some significance to him, although I never got the opportunity to find out what.

Even his face seemed to benefit from the vulnerability of his exposure. His jaw line seemed to become somewhat sharper, his cheekbones somewhat higher, and his pressing need for a more regular haircut was less obvious to the world; maybe nudity has a way of distracting us from our more common flaws? Similarly, the blue of his eyes seemed to become even more pronounced, and the increased contrast of the color of his lips against the newly smooth skin of his face made his slight knowing smile much more apparent for all to see. For those of you who care about such things, I suppose I would have to say that he didn't seem to be any more, or any less, of a man than any other. Like I said, the male nude has never held all that much fascination for me although, if I'm being honest, I will confess to an occasional element of curiosity over the years regarding how some of the men and women close to me might look in this, their most vulnerable state. James turned out to be more than I might have imagined in that respect, but let's be honest, every artist tends to flatter their subject to a certain extent, and that's probably what had happened here with the nude portrait my mother had painted of our summer guest and which she had hidden away without ever expecting me to stumble upon it as I looked through her recently painted canvases.

I can't remember what he and I talked about that day when Mary had gotten delayed and we sat in the den sipping from our teacups. I do know that I enjoyed talking to him, and I was somewhat disappointed when Mary finally arrived home and our time alone was cut short, but I'm also aware that I had a strong sense that I might not want to get too wrapped up in what he was saying to me at the time. Meeting him again last week after all these years, I realized that the man was much easier to believe than the boy had ever been. Well at least as far as I am concerned, anyway. That's not to say that the younger version of James ever came across to me as a liar, or even as just an exaggerator for that matter. Quite the opposite to be honest. It was just that the very fact that he seemed to be able to converse about virtually any subject made you wonder how he could possibly know so much, almost to the point where you would start to think that maybe the only thing that he really knew about was how to give you the *impression* that he knew something about everything? Even though you might find yourself wondering about that, it is certainly true that he never made me think that he was spinning me a line. We've all met some of those people who "must have their share of the conversation" as the phrase goes, but with James you never really felt that he just wanted to hear the sound of his own voice and, to give him his due, he was just as good at listening as he was at speaking. I guess that it was just that I was always on my guard with him a little bit because of how much I knew about his relationship with my sister and my mother.

Maybe one other thing that made the older version of James more believable is the slight sense of regret, and maybe even sorrow, which has crept into some of his words these days. The boy had always been so confident, whereas the man doesn't give you the impression that he is quite so sure of himself. Apart from that one occasion with the daycare situation, and a few stolen sentences at the end of summer party that he held at his place, I only ever heard the boy speaking in a group situation with the rest of my family around and I have found myself regretting that over the years. We all know that most men can talk all day long, but they don't really start to *say* anything until you are alone with them, and you have their trust. Maybe Mary and the boy James would lay together and he would share his fears and doubts in the aftermath of their intimacy, but for me I never heard a single word of regret pass his lips until he sat opposite me thirty odd years later and held his tiny cup of espresso in his tired looking hands. Hearing that not everything had worked out the way that he had wanted, and realizing that his confidence had taken a beating along the way, wasn't nearly as inspiring to listen to as his youthful words had been back in that summer, that's for sure, but somehow it made what he said all the more believable, and I found myself liking him even more in these more recent moments.

Chapter 7 – The Visitor

The night before the first of his court appearances my father took the most unusual step of paying me a visit in my bedroom at home. He must surely have been in my room on any number of previous occasions while I was growing up, but it was such an unusual occurrence in more recent times that I honestly couldn't think of any specific occasion. His presence in my room was so out of the ordinary that it already had me well out of my comfort zone from the moment I heard his light tap on the door and then the pause as he waited to be admitted. My mom, on the other hand, would never have paused for even a second before waltzing into my room.

After some unusually awkward initial words, he got to his point. Basically, he wanted to tell me what was most likely going to befall him at the courthouse the next day, and to let me understand his plan for what I should do if he didn't come home the following night. As you can imagine, following the days that he had spent hiding out from anyone who might be looking for him, and my growing suspicions about the nature of the business that he was involved in, I wasn't ever going to be completely surprised that he had gotten himself into "a little trouble", as he put it. What I did find rather shocking however, was the handwritten list of things he had prepared and that he wanted to discuss with me. Nowhere on that list was any indication of what he had done or what the outcome might be. Instead, he had prepared what could only be described as a hand-written ledger for the finances of our household outlining, to an astonishing level of detail, how he expected things to be if he was to be gone for any length of time. More shocking still, was his instruction that it was I who was to be the custodian and the executor of this contingency plan for the family. Me. Little Maggie. Baby Girl.

You can imagine too that I was far more caught up in the sudden realization that we might have to be a family of three for a while, and that it would be the true head of our family, the one who had so successfully shielded all three of his girls from the real world for so long, who would be gone. I wanted to know what my father had done, how it had happened, and how long we might be without him, but he clearly wasn't prepared to touch on any of those matters, preferring instead to try to tell me about how often the utilities bill would fall due and how much it was likely to be. My attempts to interrupt him were never going to succeed, even when he stopped to light his little cigar, here in my bedroom, and the strangely reassuring aroma started to fill my little sanctuary. Instead, he paused only momentarily to combine exhaling with his signature little cough before going on to tell me that he had included details on how to run the store with Marie in his absence. It remains, to this day, my most bizarre recollection of any conversation I ever had with my father. He never explicitly said that I wasn't to discuss any of this with my sister or my mother, but that was certainly clearly understood, and I knew too that I was not to even think about asking why he might have chosen me over either his wife or his first born, but I guess I was beginning to know the answer to that question anyway.

The following day, when the judge ended up sending him home and it looked like he was going to escape the pain of confinement, he didn't mention either the ledger or any of the other parts of our conversation, preferring instead to act like his little visit to me had never happened. I often wonder how our relationship might have been different if he had indeed completely escaped his brush with the law and stayed out of prison, but we'll never know the answer to that question. Later on, of course, once he got so badly hurt, our relationship changed in an entirely different way anyway. I'm sure, however, that if he had been able to give any thought to anything of consequence in those days after those guys hit him, he would have been glad that he had prepared me in the way that he thought he needed to for my new role in the family.

Once they did lock him up, my father would never agree to allow my mother to visit him whilst he was in prison. According to mom, he always told her it wasn't an "appropriate place" for a lady like her to visit. Like everything else with my dad, I did sometimes wonder what his real intent was in taking that stance, but there was still something slightly romantic in my mother's understanding that he was protecting her from the tough reality of his situation. In the end, he wasn't in the harshest of prison communities for all that long before they moved him to a much more relaxed, halfway house type of place. I'm guessing that those first few weeks in the "rough house" were all about sending him some sort of a message that life could be hard for him if he didn't co-operate but, given his age and the relatively tame nature of his crime, the authorities obviously didn't see the need to keep him there for his full term. All the same, he stuck to his principles and wouldn't let our mother visit him even when his situation was that little bit better in the open prison. He wouldn't even let her come and pick him up on the day that he was finally released for good, or when he was granted the luxury of occasional home visits in the final few weeks of his sentence. "Training for Freedom" was the name given to those home visits when he would be allowed to come home for the weekend on the understanding that he would be back at the front gates of the prison at 6am on the following Monday morning, so that they could take him back inside. Dad used to laugh at the thought that, having been free for over fifty years, he somehow had to be trained in the art of freedom after just a few short months of incarceration. He would tell us that it was all just a ruse by the authorities to cut down on the cost of prison guards over the weekends, but then, on the very few occasions that he did talk seriously about those days, he would occasionally get a sad look in his eye and let it slip that there were other guys of his age who truly needed to be trained for the new world they were coming back into after a much longer period of time inside.

So it was that my mother never saw her husband in his ill-fitting prison uniform, shuffling along with the rest of the inmates who probably had more in common with him than perhaps he himself ever wanted to believe. Mary too, was never forced into the sort of self-examination that comes to you when you see the colossus that you like to believe your father is, reduced to little more than a number, and you realize that humiliation in the eyes of those who love you is the hardest part of any sentence they might impose upon any man. My mother and my sister really have no idea about the prison lifestyle, just like they have no idea about how often I was the one who visited my father behind bars. It was all set up through his so-called friend Bud of course, and I knew from the very first time he got in touch with me that the rest of the family could never be allowed to know what was going on. Within just a few days of him being sentenced I was able to meet with him in the place that he called the "rough house". He was behind glass as you would expect, and he was speaking to me through a telephone handset that was so heavy and sturdily built that it felt like it could survive World War III. It was him all the same, my father, even in that jumpsuit that was a dozen sizes too big for him – "all designed to make us look ridiculous and heap shame upon us" according to the man himself who was quickly learning how this new game was played.

I wanted to talk about life, love, and freedom but, of course, that wasn't the reason my father had summoned me there to this place that he had decided was too much for my mother or sister to be asked to endure. He wanted to talk about money, about the bills, and about the business. I was to be the conduit through which he would continue to protect and support his family nearly as well as he always had done, and if one of his girls had to give up her innocence to protect the other two, then that one was to be me. He never explicitly told me that I was "the one" of course, and he never told me that he was looking to me to bring the family the wisdom and leadership that he couldn't for the time being. He didn't have to tell me. Or at least, he didn't have to say anything in order to tell me.

That's not to say that you should ever get the impression that I gradually came to know all about my father's affairs and all of our family secrets. Far from it. I guess I just came to know a little bit more than everyone else about a particular part of what was going on with him. Isn't that always the way of things? Nobody knows everything, and none of us really know more than anyone else. We just know *different* things from each other, and true wisdom is little more than knowing what to do with the information that you do have.

When my father finally came home for good, he wouldn't even allow mom and Mary come to the open prison to pick him up. Of course, that meant he couldn't ask me to be the one to collect him either, otherwise they might have suspected that I had been visiting him all along. Instead, he had arranged to be picked-up at the prison gates and driven by "a friend" to the parking lot of an abandoned cinema just a few miles from our home, where we were all to meet him before bringing him back the rest of the way. When the day finally arrived, we made our way there well in advance of the allotted time as you would imagine, and yet, there he was already waiting for our arrival. I watched him step forward and walk slowly towards us, looking older and somehow smaller than he ever had before. He couldn't quite manage a smile of course, but that was really nothing unusual for the man. None the less, I couldn't keep my eyes off him, and I had this overwhelming feeling that now things would get back to normal even though they never actually did. I assumed that it would have been the menacing Bud who had picked him up, and that he would have arranged to be dropped off early so that my mother didn't see who it was that had transported him. I was right about that part; he didn't want it to be known who had picked him up but that was because none of us had any idea that James and my dad were still in touch with each other at that time. It would be a long number of years before I learned that little piece of information. In the meantime, we were all just happy to have our father back, even if you couldn't say that he was fully restored to us. For his part, he was just happy to light a little cigar and laugh lightly into a little coughing spell.

I don't think I ever really knew just exactly what it was that James did with his time in the days that we knew him. Looking back, I suppose I might have had some vague idea that he was still in college and working towards his bachelor's degree, but when you meet someone during the long summer break you don't really see them quite as clearly as you really should, if you see what I mean? The vision that young people have of each other in those summer months is seen through the distorted lens that the long break creates for most students. I guess you could say the same thing about me of course. I was enjoying my last long summer high school break, which always seemed like it would last forever, until it was actually over and then you couldn't believe how quickly it had flown by. Sure, I had my little pretend job working for my father in his store, but I was still living the type of life only a teenager can in those times. With James, there was also the complication of money. How exactly was he able to afford to live alone like that if he was only a humble student? That would have been another mystery that I might have wanted to solve if it was the sort of thing that teens on summer break actually cared about.

When James told me last week that he was "still in engineering" I had one of those moments where you can't quite work out whether that was something you had always known, or whether it was a complete surprise. Maybe back then I had actually known that he was studying mechanical engineering right there in the very same university that was close by my dad's store, but I'm not sure. If I did, then I certainly wasn't smart enough at the time to give any credence to the thought that his chosen career path seemed to be completely at odds with both his personality and his conversation. Looking at the tired man sitting opposite me last week, I was filled with the notion that James was the least likely looking engineer I could ever imagine. No doubt that is down to a fair old dose of prejudice on my part since I was always guilty of pigeon-holing engineering and math majors as the ultimate nerds. To me, engineers were just mathematicians with dirty hands.

Another of my prejudices is that those guys also make up the bulk of the huge geek army that cares about motor cars, gadgets, and gizmos, on an almost spiritual level. James was never like that. If I were to imagine him replying to someone who asked him what kind of car he drove, I'm sure he was come up with a simple, dismissive response like "A blue one." In fairness to the boy, you would have to say that any such reply would never have been delivered with any malice. While I will openly embrace my own prejudices, and I will happily make as many disparaging jokes about those students as you can stand, I would have to admit that James would never run any of those kids down. He already had the level of tolerance that was to become so widespread among young people in these current days, some thirty years later. So, James may well have been an engineer by trade, but he certainly wasn't an engineer at heart. You only had to hear him that time he was talking to my dad about the merits of the old rail bridge that crosses the river on the north side of town. He and my dad were going back and forth at each other in what I suppose would be a version of the classic form v function debate, but the bottom line is that my dad was talking about a functional structure, and the boy was talking about an art form, even though they were both looking at the same thing.

For my own part, and for as long as I could remember, I had always wanted to go to school in the city. I'm not sure when I started to think along those lines, but I'm guessing it might have been from my earliest trips to my dad's store which was only a hundred yards or so from where the university campus was. For all those years I would see the students milling around and looking for all the world like the most grown up and sophisticated kids I had ever seen. Even as a very young child I wanted to be one of those students.

Now that I think about it, maybe campus is the wrong word to describe that part of the city. "Campus" suggests some kind of a self-contained community, maybe set out in the country, or out on the edge of town, where academia could live in peace, away from the stresses of real life. City based universities are, of course, nothing like that. The university in town seemed to much more of an organic part of the city itself, and you couldn't always tell where its boundaries began and ended. As the school had continued to grow up over the years, it had been forced to adopt some of the nearby buildings, and so you would have the curious sensation of walking along a tree lined residential street and finding the school of some obscure academic subject, sandwiched between two family homes. The lines were further blurred by the fact that the original student dorm building was only big enough to house the freshmen at best these days, with the residences of the rest of the students randomly scattered among the mere mortals, albeit in much more cramped conditions as scores of former family homes were turned into over-crowded, over-priced, student accommodation. In my youngest days, I didn't realize that the main buildings of the school were butted hard up against the city hospital which shared the same aging style of architecture. In truth, it was hard to believe that they were two separate entities although, in time, those lines would become blurred too. As you would expect, the hospital had a lot of young interns and trainee nurses who swelled the numbers of young people in the area and added to the youthful vibrancy of the area, almost to the point where I felt that my life wouldn't be complete until I was part of this community. I just couldn't wait to get there. Or at least, I couldn't wait to get there until the time came to actually go.

I'm pretty sure my change of heart started to develop during that summer that I worked in dad's store and James was part of our lives. Not that James himself had anything to do with it, you understand. He just happened to be a part of our circle as I was beginning to realize that what

I thought I had always wanted was not what I really needed when it finally became a viable option. When I went back to high school for my senior year that fall, I started to look a little bit further afield, and to wonder if maybe it would be better in the long run if I was to give up on the idea of commuting into town every day? Suddenly, and surprisingly, the thought of living away from home started to become far more appealing.

My father pretended that he was upset about my decision to give up on my long-held plans when I made my decision to live away from home. My mom, on the other hand, made out that she was all for the idea. In reality however, they were both lying. I could tell that my father felt it was part of his duty as the male parent to resist the idea of his youngest daughter flying the nest at the earliest opportunity, even though he really believed it would be for the best. I wondered too if his act was maybe just a little bit directed towards the audience my sister would provide? Mary was still living at home at the time and there was still no suggestion that her and Brad would ever become adults at that point. I thought about that situation too of course, but it wasn't like I was getting married before the eldest sister or anything like that. I was just moving out of the family home before she did.

In the end, it was our mother who got upset when I finally made the move, just as I always knew she would. I suppose that in some ways, I had become a little bit of a confidante to her over the past few years, and I was becoming keenly aware of how she would talk differently to me when Mary wasn't at home. I don't suppose I gave much thought to how Mary herself felt about my departure beyond the practical day to day stuff. I mean, you don't think about that sort of thing when you are that age, do you?

Your childhood home always seems to be so much smaller than you remember it when you come home for that first time after you've lived away for a while. It's a sensation that never leaves you for the rest of your life, and the walls of your childhood bedroom never seem to move as far back from each other as they were when you were a kid. It was all the way out until Thanksgiving before I made my first trip home in my freshman year, but you don't really get any sense of how everyday life has changed for those who remain in your absence when you only show up for set piece holidays like Christmas and Thanksgiving. I suppose that I started to understand things a little bit better when I came home for the long summer break at the end of that first full academic year, but it's also the case that even then, my very presence was disturbing whatever the new normal was for my parents and my sister. As a child I grew up torn between not wanting the sheltered existence that my father had created for us to ever end, and looking forward to huge watershed moments like graduation, college, and beyond. Leaving home to go to college seemed to be the starting line of a race that was run at a frantic pace compared to our previously slow-moving lives. I guess it was just good fortune that I happened to be at home for each of the three main life events that befell my father in those years. I had gotten through my freshmen year without too much trouble when he went to prison, and it was sometime later before he got hurt apparently at the hands of his business rivals. I would have liked to believe that my father's passing just after I graduated marked the tragic end of this race I was running, but in time I came to learn that it was nothing more than the completion of yet another lap in a long-distance event where the pace increases but the finish line continues to move further away.

Chapter 8 – The Office

For all that my father was such a huge part of our lives, it's still the case that his passing wasn't nearly as tough on all of us as you might well have expected it to be. No doubt the combination of his prison sentence, and then the aftermath of his injuries, had played their part in preparing us for our eventual life without him. I'm sure that everyone has their own unique opinion on what qualifies a man as a so-called "good dad," and I'm equally sure that a lot of those people would find it hard to agree that my father lives up to that title, given both his lifestyle and how he went about earning his living. I'm his daughter, so of course I'm always going say that there are lots of perfectly good reasons for him to be regarded as a fine father, not least of which is how well he shielded us from that part of his life which we didn't really need to know about as we were growing up. Mary and I lived well, and we experienced a childhood of security and innocence, albeit that it was financed through some questionable methods by a man whose greatest talent seems to have been his ability to be discreet. Here was a man whose wife relied on his every word despite her superior education, judgement, and social background. His daughters too, would hang on those same words and turn to him for advice and guidance even as our rebellious teenage years started to combine with a growing enlightenment about who and what this man really was.

To all intents and purposes, we really lost my father on the day that he got hurt, rather than on the day a few years later when his life ended. At first, of course, we had lived in hope that he would eventually make a full recovery, and that his voice would once again fill our home with that sense of calm authority that he had. We would talk to him in those early days in a way that presumed the recovery would eventually come, and in the belief that he could hear and understand every word that was being said around him. Even in our rare moments of doubt about his future, we would step away and whisper our concerns to each other in a hushed and guilty way, just to be sure that he wasn't hearing the sense of fear in our voices. Eventually of course, we would find ourselves openly talking about him as if he wasn't there, or find ourselves talking directly to him as if he was no more than a child. I was as guilty of that as everyone else although every once-in-a-while I would find myself looking at him and convincing myself that I could see the recognition at what I was saying in his eyes. Those were the worst moments of course, the ones in which you suspected he could hear and understand every word that was being said about him, and that he himself knew that this once fine man was now locked up more securely than any prison could ever have achieved. Truthfully, there was an element of charade in our grief when he finally passed, almost like that's how we thought we should behave when, in reality, all of us knew we were secretly glad it was over.

When our mother started dating again so soon after my dad had passed away it was quickly obvious to both Mary and I that her new friend had been around for somewhat longer than we might at first have thought. I'm sure that some people would have considered that even if she had met him when she initially said she did it would still have been "too soon" after her becoming a widow, so heaven knows what they would have thought if they had come to realize, as we did, that they had been seeing each other while my father was still alive. Mary and I enabled that of course, although I for one didn't realize it at the time. For a long time after dad got hurt, my mom had done little more than look after him, perhaps because she was still just as convinced as the rest of us that he would eventually make a full recovery. As time passed however, and everyone came to know but never admitted that this was now just a waiting game, Mary and I both encouraged our mother to find a little bit of time for herself. So it was that my sister and I would take turns tending to dad while mom found a little bit of a new life traveling to exhibit and sell her paintings without her husband there to advise her as he had done on every single issue since the day and hour they had first met. Frankly, she began to flourish in this unfamiliar environment, although it was strange for us to hear her talk of people and places in her life that we had no knowledge of.

I'm sure Mary was just as surprised as me, and maybe we ourselves even had some of those same "too soon" thoughts when mom told us that she had invited her friend to join us for our first Thanksgiving dinner after dad's passing. My sister and I had already talked about how to handle events like Christmas and Thanksgiving, and we had thought this would be the right time for either of us to become the family holiday hosts that our parents had been for as long as we could remember. When mom told us about her guest however, it was clear that she had no intention of relinquishing her role just yet, and we were probably so surprised by even the suggestion that she had a boyfriend that we never even discussed it any further. It was hardly surprising when Peter turned out to be a perfectly decent man, and that he might even have been regarded as the type of guy my mother "should have married" back in the day. A family Thanksgiving isn't the ideal place to get to know someone new of course, but there were some vague references to being divorced and missing his own kids at this time of year, that I made a mental note to follow up on at a more opportune moment – in just the same way that my mother herself had become expert at finding out about everyone's family background over the years. Well, everyone except James' of course.

Peter himself was pretty personable with good conversation, so much so that I took to him right away, and I was happy for my mother that she had some grown-up company. I liked him well enough that I let his remark about him and mom having gone to the Tristate Art Fair over memorial weekend slip past me without reply, with my only concern being whether or not my sister would catch on that our father had still been with us at that time. The level of comfort my mother had around this man was another sign that they were beyond the first flush of romance, and I liked how they worked together in the kitchen. Peter had already been there before we all arrived, and I was struck by the contrast that here he was being "hands on" in the kitchen instead of standing idly by and only ever offering up direction in the way that our father always would have. As well as being first to arrive, I was starting to think that Peter would be last to leave too as the rest of the family started to drift away, but then of course I finally understood that he wasn't planning to leave at all. I wasn't sure how I felt about that then and I'm still not sure I do now either. No one ever thinks about their mom in that way. Or at least, we never think about them in that way while they are still married to our father. As I drove home that Thanksgiving night, I realized that we think about nothing else once another man actually comes on the scene.

Maybe it was because we were all still clinging to the faint but unrealistic hope that our dad would make a complete recovery, but for some reason after he got hurt we decided not to do anything with his little private office in the house. The door remained closed and locked through the years when he had to be cared for while we waited in vain for the real version of him to return to us. Even then, it wasn't until some considerable time after he had passed away that the topic of what do with the office space started to be openly discussed. Mary was the one who came up with the idea that it should be converted into a new studio for our mother as a way to get her out of the basement when she was painting in the winter months. With its high ceiling and the two tall narrow windows on either side of the corner opposite the door, it did make pretty good sense to think about the office in those terms. It was certainly the case that our dad had it decorated like I suppose he imagined some regal gentleman in a Dickensian novel would have his private library decked out. In keeping with the rest of the house it had quite a dark look with its wooden paneling, stacked bookshelves, and dim lighting, but there wasn't anything that some basic re-modeling couldn't solve. The place did still hang heavy with the slightly stale scent of my father's cigar smoke, which I'm sure most people would find difficult to bear but for us of course, was the smell of security, reassurance, and a strongly protective presence.

The first order of business would be to clear the place of all the things that my dad had decided should be stored here in his secret vault, and it was obvious from the start that this would be no simple task. The whole place felt incredibly cramped just due to the sheer volume of artifacts that he had accumulated over the years. When my dad died, we had faced the task of disposing of his everyday trappings with relative ease. We didn't seem to have any trouble disposing of his clothes, his car, or even his guns, and the conversion of my parents' shared bedroom into a single woman's boudoir had passed off without any tears or other outward signs of emotion. His office, however, was to be a quite different affair.

A lot of the items he had squirreled away here in his lair were clearly things that he had come across in his business dealings, but which had struck a chord with him to the point where he obviously felt they were of more real value to him himself, rather than moving them on at a profit. As such, you could see an outline of his character reflected in his selection even though you couldn't really say there was any sort of common theme among them. I guess you would have to say that it was the sum of their parts that painted the picture of the owner of this quite eclectic collection. I had this strange fantasy that my father had somehow been able to identify the one precious item which most clearly defined the character of the deceased owner in each and every estate sale that he had ever attended, and then he had brought these items together to give their original owners a little bit of immortality, here in his tiny private library. I recognized some of them right away as items which had appeared briefly in our lives, and which I had assumed had been quickly sold on. Others I was seeing for the first time, like the long thin stiletto bladed letter opener, with its gleaming steel blade emerging from a red glass encrusted brass handle, and which held a particular fascination for me as I tried to reconcile its use for opening tender love letters with the appearance of it being the perfect weapon for a crime of passion.

More than anything else in the whole office however, it was his collection of Christmas and birthday gifts which was to take me the most by surprise, even though I knew he had all of these things. If anyone ever asked me what kind of gift my father would appreciate, that was the easiest question in the world to answer. We came to refer to the items he loved as "precious things" and if you were looking to buy him a gift, we'd all advise you to get him one of these "precious items", before going to explain that he would always prefer some item of gentleman's hardware over everything else. A brass business card holder with a solid reassuring 'click' when being closed over before being returned to the inside breast pocket of a dress jacket. A money clip fashioned from fine red leather, beautifully stitched with smooth black fabric on the inside and magnets buried within to retain the notes. A three-piece writing set featuring a fine ballpoint pen, a replaceable nib ink pen, and a propelling pencil with half millimeter leads, housed in an elegant hard case. These were the type of thing my father loved to receive. I had no idea however, that he would store them all here in pristine condition without ever deploying them for the task they were supposed to undertake. Cufflinks were a staple of course, and if you had left him to the last moment as you made your rounds of the stores on Christmas Eve, you always had those 'up your sleeve' as a surefire hit, even though I never ever saw him wear them. The thing was though, you had better take it seriously with my dad. I remember one Christmas when Uncle Isaac handed over a beautifully wrapped box to his brother which everyone knew would be cufflinks before he even started to unwrap it. And so it proved to be, except that in this case the wrapping and box gave no clue to the fact that these would turn out to be 'novelty' cufflinks featuring some random cartoon character in what my uncle thought would be a fine joke. The look my father shot his big brother left no doubt as to what he thought of that little attempt at humor.

Now here they all were. It seemed that each and every one of these precious items had been carefully stored in the thin wide center drawer of my father's writing desk. All completely unused and in what dad would refer to as "perfect mint condition". Even the velvet or leather effect boxes which housed each of them looked as if they had just left the store that sold them. True enough, there were some occasional flecks of ash from his little cigars scattered amongst the treasure, and I could imagine him opening each spring-loaded box top in turn to gaze upon the contents with his cigar still lodged between the fingers of his left hand. Did he recall who had given him each and every gift? Did he recall each particular occasion? By now I was looking for one particular box which I certainly knew would have been too large to fit in that center drawer. It didn't take long to locate it however in the lowest of the full-size drawers on the right-hand side. The box itself was still as dark blue as I remember, but the scrunched-up tissue paper inside had the feel of having been handled many times over which was very reassuring to me personally as you will come to understand. I carefully removed the contents and, although I'm probably exaggerating, it seemed that at that very moment the sun broke through the clouds and lit up his little office. It certainly still felt good to me as I looked upon the tiny fully rigged, ship-in-a-bottle, I had bought for my father for no other reason than him having let me work in the store all that summer when James was around. You know you have chosen the perfect gift when the occasion of handing it over elicits the only time your father was ever able to put into words the fact that he loved you.

I have absolutely no idea how or why Mary got it into her head that it would be a good idea to ask Brad to help us clear my dad's office. Maybe she thought there would be some heavy lifting that only a man might be able to handle, but more likely it was part of her on-going attempts at the time to develop her husband into the new head of the family. That, of course, was something that was never ever going to work for me because the guy just didn't have the strength character needed for the task. Mary knew it too I'm sure, but at the time she was probably still trying to save her marriage which had started to falter from the moment Brad stopped realizing how lucky he had been and started to think that he had to behave like someone he could never hope to be. I myself didn't see it at first, but it gradually became obvious that he had started to get a little bit bolder around the house from the moment that my dad had gotten hurt. I highly doubt he would have spoken and behaved the way he did if my father hadn't been locked away in a body that could no longer respond to the thoughts that, so we all believed, might still have been running around his head.

There was no actual heavy lifting to be done of course, save for bearing the weight of any sorrow that hung on the three of us, and Brad did nothing more than lift and lay one item after another with a disdainful sneer for each and every one. I didn't want him snooping around in my dad's sanctuary to be honest. I knew who my dad really was well enough by this time to be certain that we might not like everything we found in his office, and I for one didn't want to be sharing any of that with Mary's lame ass husband. From the moment I recognized this fear of what we might find I knew it was always going to be Brad who would come across the things that my father would never have wanted to be found.

I did wonder how I would have felt if Mary's husband had been the type of man that I would have wanted her to share her life with? How would I have felt about such a man being here, peeling back the layers of my father's character? Would I have minded him being here as much as I minded the man she actually chose? I can't be sure of course, just as I can't be sure that James really would have made her all the woman she could have been as I had often speculated. Had that come to pass of course, the rest of the family would have had to live with the secrets we could never share with Mary, or with each other for that matter, but to my mind that would have been a burden worth bearing. There were always questions about James' character too of course, but maybe you could also say that it is those very questions which made him what he was? So, I don't know how I would have felt if it had been James, and not Brad, who had come across the faded Polaroid photographs carefully stored between the pages of a fine old copy of *Aubrey's Brief Lives* that my dad had hidden away. What I do know, without a shadow of doubt, is that if had been James that had found them instead of Brad, he would have discreetly slipped them into his pocket without a word to the three women sharing the room with him. Not for James would there have been the almost gleeful recognition of my father's assistant in his store, the glamorous Marie, in all her naked glory, and I can guarantee you that he would have seen no need to point out that my father had taken these secret pictures in the very bedroom that he shared with our mother.

I couldn't say that my mother wasn't at all hurt with the discovery of the photographic evidence that proved her husband was just a man like any other, but it's certainly true that she was less upset about it than her eldest daughter turned out to be. The tawdry pictures weren't the only secrets my father had hidden away of course, but they were the most upsetting for our mom purely because she could see the hurt they brought to Mary's eyes. In her heart, Mary herself probably knew that her dad was just a man, and so I'm sure it would have been much easier for us all to put the whole thing behind us if it hadn't been for the apparent joy that Brad took in his wife's growing realization that her father hadn't been all that she had believed him to be after all.

I have no doubt that it would have been at that very moment that my mother started to think about her own legacy and how we might come to regard her after she too was gone. Like all of us however, she would put off doing what she knew she should until it was close to being too late. So it was that she started to panic a little when she had her own health scare just a year or two later and found herself in a hospital bed. In spite of her fears we all knew that she was going to completely recover, but since we weren't the ones getting all the medical attention, it was easy for us to be confident on her behalf. I could clearly see that she was becoming concerned about her own mortality, and I distinctly remember that it was a glorious sunny Sunday afternoon when I visited my mother in the hospital and found myself truly alone with her for the first time in as long as I could remember. Mary was off somewhere with her own daughters that day and would, no doubt, be tearing herself up over whether she had made the right decision to focus on her role as a mother, over her role as a daughter that day.

Mom didn't explicitly mention our discovery of my dad's somewhat darker secrets in his office that day, but I'm sure it was on both our minds as the conversation started to unfold. She wanted me to take care of "some personal items" that she didn't want Mary to know about "just in case things don't work out for me in here". At first of course, I tried to make her see that she was being over dramatic and that she would be home before too long to take care of those things herself if she really wanted to, but I began to see how important it was to her, and she was adamant that I take on the task. I started to wonder once again about the significance of the fact that it was me, Baby Girl, who was being entrusted with this task rather than my elder sister. Later that same day, I found myself in my mother's bedroom on a secret mission to spirit away any symbols of her femininity that she felt she wasn't able to share with Mary. I was obviously touched to know that she trusted me to take care of her privacy, but I think she must have known that I could never resist the temptation to read each and every one of the hand-written letters she had shared with James over the years. I was only seeing one side of their conversation of course, but I could fill in enough of the blanks to know that she had poured out just as much of herself to him as he gave her in return. As for James, well it seems that the boy could write just as well as he could talk. After all these years I can't remember too many of the actual words, but I have a pretty clear impression of what they had come to mean to each other. Two lines that do stick in my mind were when he was talking about how much he enjoyed writing to her as his "thoughts become conclusions when I write them down" and another that said something like "you can't keep a verbal conversation under your pillow at night the way you can with a letter." When our mom made the full recovery we all knew she would, I decided that I wouldn't mention either her correspondence, or any of her other private items, unless she specifically asked me about them. To this day, I'm still waiting for her to bring the matter up, but I haven't decided yet whether I'll lie when the moment comes and tell her that I disposed of everything as she had asked, or whether I'll confess and let her know that her precious boy's letters are all carefully hidden away in my home.

Chapter 9 – The Tomato Expert

The first time I had ever set eyes on James in our home, I remember that I had come out of my bedroom and walked casually along the balcony that overlooked our living area before sitting down at the top of the stairs and listening in while he entertained my mom and my sister with his music and his stories. In stark contrast however, I was standing timidly at the other end of the hallway, right outside my bedroom door, pushed back against the wall to hide my presence, while looking furtively down when I saw him in our home for what would prove to be last time. It was the day immediately after James had held his big end-of-summer party at his place, and I guess that means I'll forever have to wonder if the party itself played any part in the scene that I was watching unfold? He was in a heated but whispered conversation with my father right in the center of the wide-open space below me. It was clear that they were completely unaware that I was watching although, yet again, I couldn't hear what was actually being said. None the less, I could tell that tempers were more than a little bit frayed on both sides. No one else was around while they were going at each other until my mother appeared suddenly at the doorway leading out to her garden, and called to my father, "Tom darling, you're the tomato expert, come and look at this!" before she stepped away again just as quickly as she had arrived. In spite of the fact that it was my father she had summoned, it was to be James who made the first to move to follow her outside. I watched however, as my father grabbed the boy's arm and spun him around to face him. "What about me?" my dad demanded, having forgotten that he was supposed to be whispering. James looked at him straight in the eye and took a long pause before replying so slowly and clearly that I finally heard every word. "I don't know Tom. You're the fucking tomato expert. You tell me."

I don't suppose you could really say that James and Mary broke up with each other in the traditional sense, since they weren't really supposed to be a couple in the first place as far as everyone was concerned. In reality however, they were very much together, and so their breakup, when it came, was just as real as any other. Like a lot of family homes back in those days, our house had only one telephone, which used to sit right there in the middle of our open plan living room. If you wanted to have a private telephone conversation, then our house was not the place to be. As a result, it was unfortunate that the demise of James and Mary turned out to be a pretty public affair, with both my mother and I being within easy earshot of the unfolding events. It must have been right around the same day as the tomato expert incident, just as summer was coming to an end. Mary had gotten home from work, probably sometime around 7pm. She had grabbed a quick bite to eat from the leftovers of the sit-down meal my mom and I had enjoyed an hour or two earlier, and you could see that she had plans for the evening from the way she was eating on the move with an excited spring in her step. She was still snacking when she picked up the phone and used the old-fashioned rotary dial to call the boy. Neither mom or I paid any real attention to what was being said until the last few moments when Mary raised her voice before slamming the phone down and storming off to her room, leaving her plate with the last few uneaten bites laying precariously on the edge of the telephone table. My sister cried so very rarely in those years that when she did everyone knew that whatever the problem was it was something important, and so I wasn't at all surprised when my mom followed her upstairs a few minutes later.

For over thirty years, I had completely accepted Mary's explanation of what had happened during that infamous telephone call, and, in some ways, that made it even more of a burden for me to bear given all the family secrets that I was beginning to amass. I had played out the events surrounding the call in my head so often and had thought so much about how they had influenced our family life over the years, that I actually brought it up with James when I finally met him again. Only then did I learn that it seems their breakup was based on Mary mistakenly jumping to a conclusion for which there was no real justification. Mary had gotten it into her head that James was desperate to get her off the phone that night because he had someone else with him when she called. When my mother came back downstairs from her room and told me that Mary was hurt because James was blowing her off to be with someone else, I remember wracking my brain to try and remember where my dad would normally be at this time of night and that day of the week. Now, having spoken to James thirty years further down the line, I have no reason to doubt the man telling me that the boy wasn't with anyone else that particular night. After all, what benefit would there be in him maintaining a lie all these years later? Mary and I have both had to live with our differing misunderstandings of that telephone call in our very different ways. James for his part, seemed to be just a little bit broken by the thought that in the eyes of our family he was convicted of a crime he didn't actually commit.

As I said, until I bumped into him last week, that view of James arguing with my father was the last time that I saw the boy. Occasionally I had gotten little snippets of information about him over the years, and once-in-a-while his name would come up in random conversation at what sometimes seemed like the most surprising of occasions. Apparently, Mary and my mother had met him outside a department store in the center of town some years ago but for me, last week was our first face to face encounter since that glorious summer he spent as an almost permanent fixture in our home. My mother had told me that James had known all about my dad's condition when they had met him and, in fact, she and Mary were on the way back from visiting dad in the rest home when they had stopped in town, and so their meeting was certainly some time before my father finally passed away. They had met James purely by chance in the street and, from what I can tell, the meeting had been very friendly on all sides with no acrimony shown by Mary. By all accounts, the boy had seemed genuinely cut up about what had befallen my father, although he didn't give my mother and sister any clue about that fact that he knew much more about the whole affair than we ourselves did. Later on, I came to learn that James had also been in attendance at my father's funeral although I myself didn't see him there. He certainly didn't stand in line awaiting his turn to share a few awkward moments with us as was the tradition in those days. I can't remember who told me that he had been there and that's probably because I didn't attach any great significance to it at the time.

My mother had told me that James had looked almost exactly the same when she and Mary had bumped into him in the street that day, but when I saw him last week it was clear that time had not been so very good to the boy over the years. His hair was thinner, and his skin had a flat and dry look about it. Those hands that played the piano so smoothly were now worn and tired, with the look of having had some heavy loads pass through them. The baby blue eyes had faded to gray although you had to look closely within the deep dark pockets that housed them to be sure. It seemed that the only thing that was the same was the fact that he was still thin and athletic looking, without an ounce of extra weight.

Actually, that's not completely true, now that I think about it. His weight wasn't the only thing that had remained the same with him over the years. Even after whatever it was that he'd been through in these last three decades or so, the man still had the boy's ability to talk and hold your attention, whether you believed what he was saying or not. With him, now just as it was then, you always found yourself wanting to hear whatever it was he was going to say next.

I had met him outside a secondhand bookstore right in the heart of the city. He was coming out of the store with a package wrapped in brown paper and tied with string in a way that made it look almost as old as the books within would surely be. He was wearing a timeless pair of loose-fitting jeans, with a faded blue polo that wasn't tucked-in the way he always used to wear his shirts. That meant I couldn't see if his belt was still a perfect match to the color of his shoes as it certainly would have been back in the day. The shoes themselves were still immaculately clean and well looked after the way they always were, and I guess the whole outfit would have been pretty sharp looking when it was new, but that was obviously some considerable time ago. I myself was outside the store, in the late fall sunshine, looking through a pile of the discounted stock which the storekeeper had thoughtfully placed on a low table on the walkway in front of the store, in the hope of catching the eye of an impulse buyer or two like me. For a fleeting moment I thought I saw him hesitate just a little bit before he started to speak to me, but I might have been mistaken. To be sure, if there had been any hesitation on his part it was the first and only time I had seen that in him and, equally surely, it was gone in an instant.

Meeting and talking with him again after all this time, it began to dawn on me that the "big attraction" about James was not that he was someone who had all the answers, but rather that he was someone who raised a lot of questions. Questions about him himself of course, questions about those around him, and ultimately, questions about yourself as you listened to him speak. He really didn't have any great ability to satisfy your curiosity, but he sure knew how to pique it. Don't get me wrong. I'm not trying to suggest that this was something he did deliberately, because I'm certain that it was a completely inadvertent response. I'm also absolutely certain that he provoked a lot of questions in both of my parents and my sister too. I would often wonder if they still thought about him and the issues he caused as much as I did? Meeting him again, I began to understand that my previous views about him weren't completely accurate. You see, I had always thought that his influence on our family extended to everyone *except* me, but I'm beginning to realize that this is not exactly true. For sure, I had always known that the way I came to regard my sister, my mom, and my dad, after that summer, was influenced more than a little by him and what he brought to our family, but I wasn't as aware just how much he had influenced me in my own right. As he and I sat there in the coffee shop just around the corner from the bookstore last week, I knew that I would be leaving there with yet more questions than answers, even though he was destined to burden me with more information than I might be able to handle.

The man has certainly gotten me to thinking about how I would have felt if I had known what had really happened to my father at the time the events went down. How would I, along with everyone else who knew him, have regarded him if they had known the truth, and maybe more importantly, how has our regard of that particular truth changed in the years in between then and now? As James said, in some ways, the men who almost ended my father's life back then might be the very same type of men who would strive just as intensely to protect his life in these more modern days. Not that there is ever any good way to lose your father, of course – in those days, or in these. The passing of a parent is another a rite of passage for every son or daughter, and things are never the same after your parents are gone, but in my case, it's the manner of my father's passing that has given me pause for thought in these most recent days. The manner and the timing. How we view the manner of some events is often heavily influence by the times in which we view them.

The other unanswerable question that James has left me with is how much of all of this does my mother really know? My mother, and my sister too for that matter. It seems to me that I am still not over my long-held fascination with the idea of our family secrets that started all the way back at my cousin's wedding when I was in my early teens. Am I still the baby of the family who has been shielded so well from the real world by my late father, while everyone else knows everything that I don't? Or has Little Maggie become the custodian of our family history that my father clearly wanted me to be, to the point where I'm the only one who really knows what went on? Certainly, whether she knows or not, my mother had let me continue to believe that dad's life of petty crime had finally caught up with him, and that his so-called gangland rivals just pushed a little bit too hard the night they ended his career, and his life. As I've said many times before to anyone who asked or cared, I honestly never felt the slightest bit of shame when my dad went to prison, and I never felt any shame about the manner of his passing either, at least as far as I understood it at the time. Even now, when I finally know the truth, I can also honestly say that I still have no shame about what ultimately led to his death, and I might just allow myself to even consider him a little bit of a martyr in a noble cause, but it's also true that I am one of many among us who might not have felt that way back at the time it happened. That is to our shame, and for us to refer to them as "different days" is the weakest of our excuses.

While I might start to let myself believe that I am the one who has collected and collated the most of our family secrets over the years, I should also be prepared to admit that maybe it was a little bit naïve of me to assume that when Mary and James broke up, his presence in our family would come to a complete end. Certainly, he was no longer seen around the house, and the times when it appeared almost as if he was holding court at our family dinner table were all in the past. Traditional teenage boyfriends come and go in all families and ours was no exception, but I suppose I should never really have considered James to be in any way traditional. From what he told me recently, it seems that he and my father had stayed in touch long after that summer. James had apparently gotten involved in the family business pretty soon after my father had first taken a shine to him. It seems that he worked as some kind of a handyman for my father that summer, and he told me that he would often be sitting in the pickup truck outside the back door of the store, watching the glamorous Marie and myself leave for the day, on those occasions when my dad would come to the store late in the day. He did admit that he wasn't at all sure why my dad wanted him to keep it quiet that he was working in the family business and apparently, like me, Mary too had no clue about this job of his that my father had given him. At first, I wondered if he was lying to me about not understanding my father's reasoning and that he knew fine well why my dad wanted him to keep things quiet. In fairness to the man however, he didn't seem to have anything more to hide as we both looked back on those long-gone days.

James knew all about my father going to prison too, and it seems that he was the one who kept some of the business going while his employer was doing his time. The store in the west end closed of course, in a move that was overseen by the boy himself, but it appears that even that exercise was another little bit of a cover story created by my dad – a token gesture to try to indicate to the authorities that a particular part of my father's life was over, now that the law had supposedly caught up with him. For some reason, as James told me about wrapping up the store, and occasionally ever since, I'll wonder whatever happened to the glamorous Marie. She would be a pretty good age by now if she is still around.

So too, James knew the truth about how my father had come to meet his fate, meaning once again, that I would come to learn about my family secrets from the most unusual and slightly disturbing, of sources. He was well aware that this was no gangland warning to an old stager to let him know that his career was over. He was well aware that the young men who beat my father a little more severely than they intended that night were not in the pay of some underworld rival. He was well aware that this was the work of passionate youth, determined to show the world how they thought that men should live their lives, and to meat out punishment to those whose lifestyle didn't conform to their ideals. So, James was well aware that my father was not in any danger from any of the men who were his business associates, and that the danger he faced came from a source that had no cares about how he earned a living.

Chapter 10 - The End of Summer Party

Although I pretended that I really didn't want to go to James's party, the truth is that by the time that Mary asked me to accompany her I was already more than happy to go along and to be in his company once more. Summer was well on the way to its inevitable end, and my last year of high school was about to begin, but there was no doubt in my mind that I too had come under a little bit of the boy's spell. For sure, I had come to like him over those previous few weeks, and I enjoyed hearing him talk just as much as the rest of the family did albeit without quite getting intimately caught up with him in the way that it seems both my mother and my sister had. I suppose that in many ways James probably regarded me as the quiet one of the family since our direct conversation had always been fairly limited, but it's also the case that I had always gotten the sense that he knew I was listening to every word he said. Mary had told me that the party was going to be "no big deal", and that he was just having a few friends around to his house to mark the end of the season. She said she didn't want to go alone in case people thought that maybe her and James were a couple. I laughed out loud and asked what could possibly give them that idea? After that, I held out for just a little bit longer for the fun of being infuriating to my sister, before I finally agreed to go along with her, just like I knew I would from the moment she had first mentioned it. In truth, I liked the idea of being in his home again after our previous fleeting visit with our dad.

When we got there, his place had a very different feel from the first time, as you might well imagine. There were about ten or twelve people who had arrived before us to give the place a much busier and livelier atmosphere that it had lacked previously. The crowd made the place feel much smaller although it also felt warmer and more welcoming, with the music spilling out of the door and windows to greet us as we arrived. For all of Mary's concerns about not wanting to appear too close to, or too enamored with the boy, she sure had made a lot of effort to look her best. Her hair was pinned up at the sides around her ears and tumbled down the open back of the light summer dress she had chosen. She never wore much make up, so the little extra she had applied on that particular night was fairly noticeable to me at least, although without being anywhere near excessive. I suppose it was one of the first times that I had noticed just how much my sister was growing into being her mother's daughter, a look that her heels and dress did nothing to diminish. She certainly didn't look in the slightest bit out of place or over-dressed for the occasion, given that James's friends seemed to be a very mixed bunch with an 'interesting' range of styles and tastes.

James himself was working in the kitchen, "cooking up a storm" as he always liked to say, when we walked through the door. As he completed each dish, he would lay it on a breakfast island in the middle of the room beside the rest of the things he had already prepared. People were already eating and helping themselves to drinks from the forest of bottles which was being added to as each new person arrived. The thing that I noticed most was how relaxed everyone was, and how comfortable they all were in each other's company. I could see how much of an outsider Mary felt she was to this group, and I even got a little bit of the sense that she had worked herself up into something of an "audition mode" for this audience, but everyone seemed to know her well enough, and any initial apprehension she might have had was gone before it became noticeable. It quickly became apparent that there was no real need for me to be there to support Mary as James' friends had no issues with her at all. All the same, I was still more than happy to be there and to enjoy the fact that Mary didn't constantly need me to be at her side. I didn't really talk to many of his friends all that much, but I was never bored, and I certainly never felt in any way ignored or left out. James made sure that my glass was always topped up, but other than that he didn't single me out at all at first, which made it all the more surprising to me when one of his friends told me that James had been particularly hoping that I would come along.

Just like the previous time I had been in his home, I found myself able to wander around alone, trying to find out a little bit more about this boy from the things that he surrounded himself with. The fact that there were so many people there, and that both he and Mary were busy, meant that I could once again "fly under the radar", and I was able to float around without drawing too much attention to myself. His habit of peppering the walls with cheap reproductions of famous artworks, or portraits of their creators, seemed to extend to the whole house including the bathroom, of all places, where the illustrations he had painstakingly cut from whatever magazine had been their source, were curled at the edges from being too long in the humid atmosphere of the room. The whole house was very much a man's place, without any of the delicate touches that our mother had managed to add to our own home, despite the overwhelming influence that my father had on how and where we lived. I can't remember how it was I came to learn that James didn't either own or rent the place but that it had come into the possession of his family when some distant relative had passed away and bequeathed it to them. The family apparently didn't want to part with the place, but it was equally clear that they also didn't want to completely pass it on to James, since he was only allowed to make very superficial changes to it.

Apart from his hi-fi system, there really wasn't that much in the way of technology, from what I could see. He didn't seem to have a computer anywhere in the house, which wasn't all that unusual back then, but the lack of a television was certainly a little bit surprising. You could tell that the kitchen was the most important room in the house as far as he was concerned, although, like everything else, it was also clear that he would have wanted it to be so much more than he was allowed make it. Maybe that was why he enjoyed cooking in the huge galley kitchen at our place so much?

As the party continued to get busier, it became even easier for me to blend into the background and to continue my exploration. His bedroom door was the only one in the whole house that was completely closed over, and so it did take a little bit of time for me to become bold enough to turn the handle and check it out. It turned out to be the largest, but yet the least impressive room in the whole house. There was a huge double bed, which hadn't been made up that particular day, but which still wasn't the wild mess you would expect of a lot of young men. The thing that made this room stand apart from all the rest was the fact that there wasn't a single picture on the any of the walls. There were the fewest signs of his personality here in this, the most personal part of the house. The bedding was of some non-descript pattern that would only ever have been bought by a woman for a spare bedroom when she was expecting distant relatives to visit from out of town. There was a walk-in closet and a small bathroom off to the side which was painted completely white with all the personality that suggests, and I could see nothing in particular in his selection of male potions or lotions that would set him apart from any other man I knew. I liked the traditional style razor hanging on a stand with a matching shaving brush but in truth, the only question that came to my mind as I checked out his bathroom was whether or not everyone else looked inside their hosts' mirror door cabinets the way I was prying into his? Occasionally I would get the impression that the bedroom did have a faint odor that wasn't particularly pleasant but which for some reason I found to be both oddly familiar and reassuring, but it was so fleeting that I couldn't quite place it. I can't remember the title of the book on his nightstand, but it was laid facedown open at his page, in what seemed to be a signature mark of the boy. The digital alarm clock was an already old-fashioned model even back then - it was one of those in which the numbers are a series of cards which flip over with each passing minute. I'm sure James would have told me that it was "retro" or a "design classic" if he had seen me smiling at it. On the floor at the far side of the bed, farthest from the door, there was a small tea plate which I could see had been pressed into service as a makeshift ashtray, perhaps to be used by an unexpected visitor to his nocturnal lair. As I stepped a little closer to it, I could see that the source of the faint but reassuring scent I was catching was two small cigar ends which his bedroom guest had left behind.

With my heart still racing in this moment of realization, I tried to close the door as gently and as quietly as I could before making my way back to the rest of the party guests. My efforts were in vain however, because when I turned around, he was standing there looking straight at me with a slight smile on his face. I pretended to be more embarrassed about being found out than I really was, and I said something about "just being my usual nosy self", but I could tell right away that he didn't mind in the slightest that I had been snooping around his bedroom. In fact, we both joked about it as I confessed that I was really more upset that my much-vaunted ability to move around a crowded space without being noticed wasn't quite as strong as I had convinced myself it would be. He told me to come join him in the kitchen so that we could talk, "while I'm being creative" as he put it, and I like to think he enjoyed my flirty question in reply about whether it would be his cooking, or his conversation, that would be the creative part. Despite my thoughts to the contrary it was clear that he had actually noticed my wandering around right from the moment I had arrived, and how I seemed to be taking everything in. He wanted to know if I was ready to share what kind of picture I had formed of him in my head as I had looked around his home. I told him that I would need to know the answer to a few more questions I had before I was ready to do that. As I spoke, I knew full well he would never be able to resist my prompting him into inviting me to ask my questions.

"Well firstly, I want to know if the reason that you lay your books face down, open at your place, is to fight off a long-standing habit you had as child of folding down the corner of your page? In my mind I'm pretty sure that's true, but I just don't know if you yourself realized that page folding is a nasty habit, or was it just that it disappointed your little old mother?" I teased. "Oh, that's a great question" he beamed, "but I'm going to have to ask for time to think up a suitable reply which is just as imaginative! A question as good as that one deserves something more than just the plain old truth for a reply, don't you think?" I was happy to grant him his time to think but only on the condition that he was going to have to come up with instant answers for the rest of my questions. So it was that I got rapid fire comebacks on my queries about the fact that none of the scores of pictures on his walls were family shots, whether or not the jazzy looking guitar was a showpiece or he could actually play, and a whole host of others in which I knew I was just toying with him as

I tried to work out exactly how much I was prepared to take advantage of this invitation to quiz the boy. In truth, I didn't know if I was brave enough to ask the question I really wanted to ask.

In the meantime, it was fairly clear that Mary was doing her very best to "work the room" as they say. She seemed to be trying to make sure that she spoke to everyone and, like all of those who have mastered the fine art of diplomatic conversation, I could see she was giving everyone she spoke to the opportunity to talk much more often than they had to listen to her. Her preoccupation with making a good impression on James' friends had the benefit of giving me more time than I could have hoped for to talk to the boy, but when she saw me still deep in conversation with him more than twenty minutes after her previous searching glance, I knew that my time of having him all to myself would be over shortly, and that she would be coming to join us before very long.

I'm honest enough to admit that by this time I was more than a little bit disappointed to realize that our private conversation was coming to a premature end, but I decided to try and turn it to my advantage by leaving him with a question that I knew he couldn't hope to answer before we two became a three. For all the wisdom he had beyond his tender years he still couldn't avoid the honey trap I had set and I'm sure he wasn't in the slightest bit aware that Mary was about to join us when he asked enthusiastically "So what else do you want to know, little girl?" In a perfect world I would have had more time so that I could have made something out of a mock sense of being insulted about being called "little girl", and I was already a little bit upset that I was going to have to cut my line of questions around being curious about where he hid the piano he used to give my sister her lessons. Instead, I could feel my heart beating a little faster as I began to wonder if I really was bold enough to ask my next question. "Well James, this particular '*little girl*' wants to know who it is that smokes those little cigars in your bedroom?" I didn't get enough time to watch his reaction before turning to respond to Mary's playful opening question of "What are you two co-conspirators talking about while you leave me to entertain all the other guests?".

Chapter 11 – Bella Donna and the New Tomato Expert

"I used to call you 'Bella Donna'" he said with a gentle laugh and down turned eyes which still couldn't mask the obvious pleasure of the memory. "This was back before I had any idea of what your real name was, although I still loved that name once I was lucky enough to come to know you in person. Even now, you are still 'Bella Donna' in my dreams. I loved that you had that whole gypsy look going on, in a way that set you so far apart from everyone else as far as I could see". I was thrilled at the thought of a compliment delivered thirty years after the fact, but I couldn't help but play it down by telling him that Bella Donna was also the name given to a toxic plant better known as Deadly Nightshade, and that perhaps he didn't know what he would have been getting himself into. He paused before another gentle smile and a faraway look gave me the impression that he was enjoying this little piece of information I had shared with him, given that he had always been the one with the background knowledge in the past. He was looking straight at me now and even though he was sharing his long-held feelings for me I was suddenly struck with the realization that this man's charm was in his ability to share his knowledge, experience, and stories, without ever having even the slightest air of superiority.

I understood, of course, that the age difference between us back then would have been considered significant, and an almost certain road to trouble, but now of course, those few years are nothing as we have both wandered into middle age. I suppose in some ways it was more than a little bit disconcerting to know that he had been watching me from afar all those years ago, but in other ways I might just have felt good about it at the time, to be honest. Young teens have a certain craving for the attention and the approval of the borderline twenties. I'm sure it would have been a huge boost for me back then, and I would have almost certainly have enjoyed his apparent admiration thirty years ago. Maybe just as much as I enjoyed his attention last week.

"You looked so slight and so delicate back then that I got it into my head that I alone could protect you. I have no idea where I got the crazy notion that I could get closer to you by dating your sister!" he laughed. "I guess it worked out in the end though, because I got to know the man who really did protect you from this world better than anyone else ever could." His eyes were filling up now, but he fought off his tears and confessed, "In the end it was your father himself that needed protection, and I wasn't willing to give it to him. I left your dad at the mercy of those boys who couldn't put up with men like him back in those days. Our world has come a long way since then, little girl, but that only serves to make me more intolerant of the man I was back then. I left him Maggie."

Despite my shock at what I was hearing, and the realization that not only did he know what had befallen my father, but that he was actually there at the time, I tried to offer up some kind of support in the way that you automatically do when someone bears their soul to you. I tried to tell him that it was understandable. I tried to tell him that they were outnumbered, and that getting away was absolutely the right thing to do. I tried to help him justify the boy to the man. He finally gave up on his well-developed art of looking you straight in the eye as he spoke, and he let his gaze drop to the surface of the table we were seated at. He let out a little laugh that sounded for all the world like a resigned sigh and took a long pause before he spoke. "You don't understand, do you? Neither your dad or I ever ran away from a fight in our lives. I knew that your dad could take care of himself from the first moment that I met him. I didn't run away from the fight. I ran away from the defense of a life that very few chose to try and understand back then. I didn't run away from the fight, little girl. I ran away from doing the right thing".

I don't suppose I'll ever really know how much my mother and Mary know about each other's relationship with James, or the bizarre complication that my father could add to the mix if they were ever to learn the truth. It's not exactly the type of thing you bring up in casual conversation. Whatever each of them knows, or believes, it doesn't seem to have come between them and, if anything, they've grown ever closer to each other over the years, perhaps to the exclusion of myself to a certain extent. I guess that's part of the price you pay for looking towards the horizon as often as I did over the years. In due course Mary developed the wisdom and experience that had eluded her in the classroom, and my mother and I learned to marvel at her natural ability as a parent. Mary's own daughters rode out her separation and divorce from Brad with a combination of their natural childish resilience, and their mother's careful nurturing. Those girls are very close to their grandmother, almost to the point where I might just admit to a little bit of jealousy that my own kids don't share that with my mom. I suppose that's got a lot to do with the fact that my mother would look after Mary's girls while she, as a newly single parent, continued to work and would eventually go on to develop her own chain of well-regarded private childcare centers all across the state.

It's also hard to think of your mother as having re-invented herself into a new character from the woman you had always hoped she would be forever. With a new man in her life, a style of her own in her painting, and an ever-changing role as a mentor to her growing granddaughters, I am glad that she still has that little garden, to remind us all that this is still the same woman at heart. The garden itself doesn't ever appear to change all that much. Sure, the summer furniture might have been replaced once or twice over the years, but other than that, the only other changes follow the natural cycle of the seasons.

Last fall I found myself back at home and admiring the ease with which Mary's girls occupied the same space that had been the center of the world for my sister and I not so very long ago. I smiled gently to myself as Amy, Mary's youngest, let me know that she would always stay in my blue room whenever she slept over at her grandmother's. I followed her through the house as she made her way to the kitchen and then out into the garden where her elder sister and my mother were lost in their own little world in which harvesting tomatoes was their only concern. I stopped in the doorway, neither in the house nor in the garden, and angularly leant on the doorframe in an unintended tribute to the man whose voice I still expected to hear offering up his advice at any moment. Mary's elder daughter was grasping each tomato in turn and pulling them off the vine so vigorously that the whole bush and its support frame would shake back and forth. Without the slightest hint of ire, my mother moved closer to her and, with one hand holding the vine, she gently harvested the brightest red tomato I had ever seen with the other, softly whispering to her granddaughter as she did so, "Here, let me show you".